THE FORESTWIFE

'And what well is this?' Mary asked, dreading the answer.

'Why, this is the Old Wife's Well, what else?'

Mary crumpled down beside the ancient carved stone trough, her baggage falling at her feet. 'Why have you brought me to this place? They say that those who pass this well are following the secret path. They go to seek the Forestwife deep in Barnsdale Forest.'

'Aye, they do say that, don't they.'

Mary rose to her feet again, angry now.

'How dare you bring me here? This is a place of evil. All decent folk who dwell in Sheaf Valley live in fear of the Forestwife. She's a witch of the worst kind. She blights the crops with curses and spells, and nobody is safe from her.'

Whitby

Baytown

Rosedale

Pickering

ROYAL
FOREST of
GALTRES

York

Wakefield   Wentbridge   Howden

Pontefract   Tickhill

BARNSDALE WASTES

Grimsby

Forestwife's
clearing

Sheffield
Town   Langden
Loxley   Magdalen
Holt   Sheaf Valley   clearing

ROYAL FOREST
of
SHERWOOD

Lincoln

Nottingham

THE
FORESTWIFE

Theresa Tomlinson

RED FOX

A Red Fox Book

Published by Random House Children's Books
20 Vauxhall Bridge Road, London SW1V 2SA

A division of Random House UK Ltd
London Melbourne Sydney Auckland
Johannesburg and agencies throughout the world

Copyright © 1993 Theresa Tomlinson

3 5 7 9 10 8 6 4 2

First published in Great Britain 1993 by Julia MacRae

Red Fox edition 1995

Printed and bound in Great Britain by
Cox & Wyman Ltd, Reading, Berkshire

RANDOM HOUSE UK Limited Reg. No. 954009

Papers used by Random House UK Limited
are natural, recyclable products made from wood grown in
sustainable forests. The manufacturing processes conform to
the environmental regulations of the country of origin.

ISBN 0 09 926431 5

Contents

'She waited and waited, leaning against a tree, and as she stood there it seemed to her that the tree became soft and yielding, and lowered its branches. Suddenly the branches twined around her, and they were two arms. When she turned to look, the tree was a handsome young man, who held her in his arms.'

from 'The Old Woman in the Forest', *Grimms' Tales for Young and Old*, translated by Ralph Manheim (Victor Gollancz Ltd, 1979)

1

Ecclesall Woods

Mary stood before her uncle's chair on the raised dais at the end of the great hall. Her hands shook as she twisted the heavy garnet ring that she wore on her forefinger. It had belonged to her poor disgraced mother, Eleanor de Holt. It was all that Mary had left of her, and she wore it constantly, even though it was too big to stay in place on any of her other fingers. She worked it round and round frantically until she saw that her uncle was watching, irritated by the nervous, childish action.

The lord of Holt Manor tapped his fingers on the carved wooden armrests.

'Heaven knows, child, I have done my best by thee. I pray you'll not disgrace me.'

'But Uncle . . .' she whispered her protest.

'What? Speak up, child. Speak clear.'

Her uncle bent forward, frowning with the impatience that he clearly felt.

'Uncle, he is so . . . old.'

'No good fussing and fretting about that. 'Tis what a girl child's reared for, marriage and breeding. Gerard de Broat is a grand match for a fatherless wench like thee. For my poor dead sister's sake tha must curb thy temper and

1

accept my decision. I've more to worry about than maiden's fears, what with King Richard demanding high taxes for his crusade, and now Count John is wanting men and horses to strengthen his garrison at Tickhill Castle. I swear he's arming it against his brother's return, and here am I expected to deal out money to both these warring Plantagenets.'

Mary clenched her fists and her cheeks grew red with the helpless rage that rose in her.

Owen de Holt's patience was at an end. 'You are fifteen years old, girl. Many a maid is married at twelve. Go speak to thy aunt. 'Tis her job to calm thy fears, not mine.'

He rose from his chair, and strode out of the hall, calling for his groom.

It was early in the afternoon when Mary let herself out through the back porchway into the kitchen gardens. She carried her warmest cloak, though the month was June and the sun was hot on her head and cheeks. She pressed her elbow against her side to check that the loaf of bread was still there, covered by the cloak.

Despite the desperation that she felt, there came a twinge of excitement. She was doing her best to think clearly and act wisely. She had the fur-lined cloak for sleeping and bread so she'd not starve. Her stomach churned with fear, but she made herself walk slowly through the garden. She must give the appearance of a sad but resigned young woman, taking a stroll in the fresh air. There must be no outward sign of the rage that tightened her throat, threatening to choke her. She reached the end of the rows of beans and peas, close to the small lydgate, that led to wooded pasture land beyond.

Owen de Holt and his groom suddenly clattered out on horseback from the stable yard, and Mary froze. She bent down to the soil, as though examining the swelling pods with sudden interest. But she needn't have worried, her uncle glanced in her direction, shrugged his shoulders and trotted out through the main gateway, heading towards Sheffield Town.

Mary breathed her relief. She was close to the gate now. All she had to do was go through it. She lifted the iron sneck that held it, hesitating. The garden was quiet, her aunt, Dame Marjorie, would be dozing in her solar.

Still she paused. What of Agnes? How could she go without Agnes? Without even saying goodbye! She'd been in such a state that she hadn't stopped to think.

Agnes had come to Holt Manor to nurse Mary as a baby. Eleanor de Holt had died, far away in a convent, giving birth to her daughter. Owen de Holt told Mary how he had buried his sister with many a tear of shame, then brought her tiny child back to Holt Manor, to rear her as his own. He'd called for a wet nurse for the babe, and it was Agnes who'd come asking for the job. She'd been like a mother to Mary ever since.

A door opened and a chorus of joyful gruntings greeted the kitchen maid as she scraped the vegetable peelings into the pig sty. If Mary went back now to speak to Agnes, this quiet moment would be gone. There might never be another chance so good. If she told Agnes she was running away, she'd only fret and grumble, and she'd probably insist on coming too. How would Agnes fare with her rheumaticky joints? Her nurse was not so very old, but lately she'd grown vague and forgetful. She'd even taken to wandering off for hours at a time, returning late and seeming puzzled at the darkness. No, taking Agnes could only bring them both to grief, and it would be kinder and safer not to tell her at all. If she knew nothing, she could say nothing.

Mary lifted the sneck of the gate and looked out through the orchard, and down the sloping wooded hillside that gave Holt Manor its name. The main track ran beside the river Sheaf, up past the cornmill, and on towards Beauchief

3

Abbey. She daren't go that way, the track was always busy with pack horses and travellers; some who'd likely know her as Owen de Holt's niece.

Maud and Harry who worked the mill had known her since she was a baby. They'd help her now, she knew that, but her uncle would see them turned out of the mill should they be found to give her aid. It wouldn't be fair to go to them.

She'd have to go the other way, and take the small path that led to the wooded land to the south, belonging to Ecclesall Manor. There was more hope of passing unseen in amongst the trees than on the open pathway.

Mary reminded herself of the reason for her flight and shuddered — marriage to an elderly widower, who had rotten black stumps of teeth, and smelt of sour ale and saddle grease.

She slipped through the gate and ran.

Once she had started, she dared not stop. She dared not even look back over her shoulder, but hurtled down the smooth-trodden pathway, keeping to the trees and bushes wherever it was possible. Her soft leather slippers made no sound on the warm springy earth. There was an open patch of land just before the opening in the palings, the dividing line that marked the edge of her uncle's demesne. Mary crossed it with growing speed and panic, her cloak flapping heavily and awkwardly at her side.

Her footsteps slowed once she'd reached the shelter of the trees. This was Ralph de Ecclesall's land, and she was by no means safe on it. She'd have done better not to run down the hillside, a dignified walk would have been much less suspicious, but she'd done it now and no help could come from regrets. She made herself hurry along the path that they took when she came buying charcoal with Agnes.

Ecclesall woods were not frightening like the thick, dark

forests and wild wastes. They were networked with paths, and peopled with workers. Charcoal-burners lived in hovels that they raised in the clearings, close to where they fired their bell-shaped wood stacks. Families of coal-diggers, their skin grey with the dust, worked in small groups wherever the coal seams touched the surface. The clang and clatter of iron-workers rang through the trees. They made their bloom hearths close to the streams that they dammed and used as cooling ponds.

Mary hurried on, but whenever she heard voices or the clank and thud of folk at work she turned away and went in the opposite direction. Soon she'd strayed far from the main pathway. These folk who gleaned their living from the woods owed tithes and labour to the Ecclesall Manor. Yet they had a reputation for being awkward and independent. Mary could not know if they would betray her, should they glimpse her flight. They lived on the edge of starvation, she knew that well enough, and no doubt they'd earn themselves a rich gift from Owen de Holt for the return of his ungrateful niece. She managed to avoid meeting anyone face to face, but the feeling grew in her, that maybe she was being followed . . . the rustle of leaves, the crack of a twig.

Once she jumped and trembled at a sudden shaking of the undergrowth, but it was only one of the small pigs that roamed free in the woods. It ran away squealing and snorting in the grass, to root for acorns and beechmast. They were tough scrawny things, those pigs, not like the fine fattened swine of Holt Manor, and they were harmless enough.

The going became more difficult, her feet ached, and her fine-stitched slippers did nothing to protect her from the fallen holly leaves or the sharp stones that rutted the paths. She was hot and tired and worried that she was stumbling around in circles, when she came upon the pool.

A stream tumbled white foaming water into a deep pool, surrounded by ferns, mosses and long grass. This was no iron-workers' dam, but clean fresh water. Just the sight of it made her realise how thirsty she was, and she threw herself down at the edge, cupping her hands to drink.

Her thirst satisfied, she spread her cloak and sat down, bathing her aching feet in the cool water. A slow feeling of contentment took the place of fear. The sun found its way through green willow branches, and warmed her head and hands. She tore at the loaf of bread and ate with relish. The long meals at her uncle's board had never tasted as good as this. Here she was, alone in the woods, but safe and warm, and dabbling her feet in a pool surrounded by plants, as pretty as any lady's bower.

What if she was lost? Didn't she want to be lost, lost from her uncle and the strict protection of Holt Manor? Though he and Dame Marjorie had never had children, Mary doubted that she'd really been raised as their own. She'd not been beaten, and she'd lived a comfortable life with good and dainty food, and fine clothes. Yet always there'd been the burden of disgrace. Her uncle never failed to remind her: she was baseborn. She must live in gratefulness and shame.

Mary sighed happily, and smiled. She was free of that for ever. She would protect herself now. She would be the lady of the woods.

Agnes had told her many stories when she was small. Her favourite story had been the tale of the green lady, the beautiful spirit of the woods, who walked through the forest, blessing the trees with fruitfulness, hand in hand with the green man.

Mary realised with a jolt that the sun had dropped to the horizon. She had no idea how long she'd been sitting dreaming and dabbling her feet in the pool. How could she have sat there so, letting her mind drift away with woodsprites and fairies? Her uncle or aunt might be discovering just now that their niece had vanished. Before long the light would fade. She must travel much further, and find somewhere safe to pass the night.

She pulled her feet up quickly, spraying water over her cloak. As she shifted, she caught a similar movement from the corner of her eye. Mary turned sharply towards the quivering branches. A face stared back at her, half-hidden by a leafy bush.

Mary jumped to her feet, snatching up her cloak.

'Who is it? Who is it that spies on me so?'

A young girl withdrew from the bush, pulling herself awkwardly to her feet. She couldn't have been older than Mary herself, and she looked terrified.

'I'm sorry, er . . . m'lady. I never meant you no harm.'

Mary hesitated. It was true that the girl looked harmless enough, but there'd be nothing to stop her telling what she'd seen. The girl backed away, frightened by Mary's fierce frown.

'Stop!' Mary bellowed. Then more gently, 'Stop for a moment, and let me think clear.'

The girl's cheeks were smeared with red strawberry juice, and she clutched a wicker basket, half-filled with the tiny woodland fruits. She was thin and pale, but Mary caught her breath as she saw and understood . . . the worn gown was pulled tight across the girl's stomach.

'With child?' she murmured.

'Aye,' she flinched as she answered.

Mary clicked her tongue, exasperated by the situation. Why did she have to be caught out by this pathetic creature? The sight of the swollen belly on the childlike frame brought echoes of her own fears. She stared down at the half loaf that had fallen to the grass when she got to her feet. She picked it up and handed it to the girl.

'Thanks,' she muttered, and fell to tearing at the bread

with her teeth. Mary sighed, and wrapped her cloak around her shoulders.

The girl suddenly paused in her eating, looking down at the small basket of wild strawberries. She held them out, offering them to Mary.

'For thee. Aye . . . for thee.'

Mary tried to keep back the condescending smile that touched her lips. As if she, Mary de Holt, should have need of such a thing. Still, the gesture was kindly meant, and the quiet dignity with which the girl presented her gift hinted at friendship between equals, even loyalty. Mary remembered that she had great need of both those things. She took the basket and smiled her thanks.

'Do you know who I am?'

'Aye. I think I do.'

'Should Owen de Holt come looking for me, I pray you'll not tell.'

The girl's eyes opened wide.

'I will swear that I have never seen thee.'

'Will you show me where this pathway leads?'

The girl didn't answer straight away, but continued to stare, then she walked slowly towards the earth-trodden track and Mary followed. At last she pointed ahead, and spoke.

'If thee follows this path, 'twill lead thee to a place where four ways meet. The uphill path will take thee to Ecclesall Manor. Straight on will lead to the bridge on the Totley brook. The downhill slope shall take thee towards the Abbey of Beauchief.'

Mary thanked her with growing respect. She wished she possessed such knowledge of the land.

'I go back to my home now,' said the girl. 'I shall never know which way tha went.'

She set off back along the path towards Holt Manor without ever glancing back.

Mary stared after her for a moment, then turned and hurried on to the meeting of the paths.

2

St Quentin's Well

Mary did not hesitate for long at the crossing. There would be no help at Ecclesall Manor and beyond the village of Totley lay the dangerous edges of Barnsdale Wastes, that vast and frightening wilderness that stretched for miles and miles. She took the path that led to Beauchief Abbey with the idea in her mind that a church might offer sanctuary.

The light was fading fast as the great soaring walls of the newly built abbey came into sight. Mary pulled up the fur-lined hood and gathered her cloak tightly around her. The summer evening had turned chill and she felt urgent need of a safe, warm place to sleep.

She crossed the wooden bridge over the river Sheaf and climbed the gentle slope towards the abbey, keeping close to the trees. The nearer she got, the more her doubts grew. How would they receive her, those austere white canons? She'd heard of folk accused of crime claiming the right to sanctuary, but they'd been men. Would the same apply to her?

Something at the back of her mind nagged away, increasing her distrust. Solemn chanting drifted in waves of sound across the fish ponds and fields. Of course . . .

she remembered, the monks had come from France, they chanted in Latin and spoke the Norman tongue.

Mary moved along the edges of the wooded land, gratefully eating the tiny, sweet strawberries, watching the cloister doors. The candle glow in the stained-glass windows promised warmth and safety. There'd be guest rooms, a warm fire and good plain food. Her stomach told her that a handful of strawberries was not enough.

A fine carved statue stood in a niche beside the door. A Virgin and child, another Mary, one hand raised in blessing. Surely there was safety here. She took a step towards it, then she stopped, trembling. The carved stone face was blank. No blessing there at all — the hand was raised in warning. Stop! Go back! Run away!

With a fresh sense of fright, Mary gathered up her skirts and shrank backwards amongst the trees. Before she'd had a chance to move far into the shadows, the clattering of two horsemen made her turn in alarm. They rode at great speed, spurring their horses and shouting to each other, but drew to a sharp halt before the abbey door.

'Open up! Open up! A message from Owen de Holt.'

Mary knew the voices. They were her uncle's grooms. She did not stay to see how they fared with the canons, but turned and stumbled on through the surrounding woodland.

She ran wildly now, not thinking of the way, but going where the trees grew thickest. She did not stop, even though her legs banged against tree stumps and scraped on rocks. Fast uphill she went, borne onwards by the energy of fear. It was only as the trees grew taller and more spaced that she slowed her steps. She must stop at last, for her legs were growing numb. She staggered on, stiff-limbed, her head drooping in despair. What had she done? She could not go back, but dare she go on? She was heading towards the place she'd feared most to go. The wilderness of Barnsdale, beyond the reaches of the law.

There were others who'd been this way, that was well known. They took refuge here, those who'd killed, or robbed, or maimed. Why, even Agnes's nephew was one of them. Perhaps he hid here still.

Mary's knees gave way and she fell to the ground. Huge great sobs shook her body. She howled like a baby in the quiet woods, careless of the sounds, or of who might hear. At last, calm came from sheer exhaustion. As her sobs grew hushed and stillness returned, she began to hear other sounds . . . delicate sounds. The rustling of small bodies in the ferns, the screech of an owl, a faint trickle of water. Agnes had told her of St Quentin's Well and promised to take her there. Fresh, clean water that bubbled from the rocks. Folk made special journeys there. It promised a safer place in this fearful wilderness.

Mary pulled herself to her feet, and followed the gurgle and murmur of the stream. A bright moon came out from behind the thick clouds, and the chill wind dropped. She found the spring, sparkling and gleaming as it ran from the rocks. It was cold and reviving as she cupped her hands to drink. There in the moonlight was a fairyland of glittering water and fern. Her spirits rose. Perhaps there was still hope for her. She crawled beneath the thick drooping branches of a yew tree close to the water's source and fell asleep.

The familiar warbling sound of a low-pitched voice humming and singing woke Mary from her sleep. She smiled for a moment, thinking that she must have had a strange dream, but then her eyes flew open and she flinched, blinded by the beams of bright sunlight that picked their way through the branches of the yew tree.

Dark green patterns and sharp mottled light bobbed above her, and a soft, bitty mass of dried yew needles covered the palms of her hands. It was no dream — she lay beneath a tall tree, but still there was the singing.

Agnes's deep croaky voice had woken her every morning since she was a child and now here it was, beside St Quentin's Well.

Mary sat up, scraping her head on the lowest sheltering branches. She rubbed her eyes to see clearer, for she could scarcely believe what she saw, and what she smelled made her dribble with hunger.

Agnes crouched before a fire of smoking beechwood, cooking big flat mushrooms threaded carefully onto sticks.

'Agnes!'

Mary crawled towards her bleary-eyed, her braided hair knotted up in tufts and spiked with yew needles and pink yew flowers.

'What!' cried Agnes. 'Is this a forest fairy, or a fierce wicked sprite?'

Mary smiled, and burst into tears.

'What a greeting,' said Agnes, pretending to grumble, 'and here's me tramping up hill and down dale to find thee, with a great bag of food and victuals on my back.'

Then, suddenly, the joy that had burst on Mary was gone in a flash of doubt. 'I'll not go back, whatever you say. I'd rather die.'

Agnes pulled a sour face and wagged her finger. 'Whatever art thou thinking, lass? Don't you know your old nurse better than that? I'd rather die than take thee back. Do you think I fed thee as a babe, and taught thee all I know, to provide a breeding sow for a rich old hog?'

Mary gasped. 'You think I've done right then?'

Agnes sighed, and flexed her stiff fingers.

'I was making my own plans. Perhaps I should have told thee. I never guessed tha'd go galloping off like a furious colt at the first sign of a bridle. Well now, let us eat these fine mushrooms that I've discovered. I shall be cursing thee if tha sits there arguing and lets them burn.'

Mary watched hungrily as Agnes drew a fresh-baked loaf from a great linen bundle and offered her golden

singed mushrooms and a hunk of bread. She ate as
though she'd never seen food before. It was only when
she'd finished the last mushroom and drunk from St
Quentin's Well that she could manage to get out more of
the questions that she needed to ask.

'But how did you find me, Agnes?'

'Huh. Tha's left a trail like a thousand snails. No, don't
go alarming. Not a trail that Owen de Holt could follow,
but clear enough to me and those that have eyes to see.'

'But . . . who else?'

'Oh . . . while your uncle went a-banging and a-bellow-
ing round the manor, and a-calling out his grooms and
horses, the kitchen maid set me on thy track. They think
you're a silly spoilt brat — oh 'tis true, they do. No need to
pull that face — but they've no love for their master and
they wish you no harm. Then the charcoal-burner gave
me the nod, though I had terrible trouble with that daft
daughter of his. Not a word could I get from her.'

'Ah, that girl.'

'She'd tell me naught, though I could see she knew. So I
puzzled a bit where the paths all meet, but I know my girl
and I remembered how you wished to visit St Quentin's
Well. So here we both are, but we cannot stay. We must be
on our way.'

'Where?' begged Mary. ' 'Tis all very well to say go, but
who will give us help and shelter? Everyone fears my
uncle.'

'Aye, here they do, sure enough, but I know where to
go, my lovey. Just trust me and follow me, and though
we've a long way to go, we shall be safe by nightfall. Now,
tha might help to share my burden, for I didn't leave in
such a rush and thought well what might be needed.'

Mary opened her mouth to tell how she'd been careful
to bring her cloak, but she closed it again and said
nothing. Agnes rooted in the bundle and pulled out a
strong pair of riding boots.

'I took these from the youngest groom. I guessed they'd fit thee well enough. He went tearing round in circles in his bare feet, cursing and swearing when the master ordered him out to search.'

Mary looked down at her slippers, they were in shreds. Torn ribbons of the soft leather trailed from her feet. She took the boots gladly and pulled them on. She'd never worn anything so heavy on her feet before and they felt strange and clumsy, but her toes grew warm.

A dark red kerchief, the colour of fallen leaves, came next from the bundle.

'Tie this around your head, like me. Aye, do it yourself . . . you must learn, for I've more to do now than act as lady's maid.'

Mary flinched at the sharpness, but she did as she was told with a flush of shame. None of these things had entered her head.

'Kilt up thy gown, aye, that's right, like the maid that carries the slops. Now tha's more fit to go striding through the woods. Pack away that fine purple cloak, we shall have to change that. I've another good wool cloak in here to make up a bundle for thee. See what I've thought to bring. Two sharp knives, a bundle of the strongest twine, needles, best tallow candles and a tinderbox and flint.'

'All right, all right,' Mary gathered the goods into her bundle. 'Tha's wonderful, Agnes,' she said, a touch sour. 'I'd be lost without thee.'

They filled two flagons with the cool clear water from St Quentin's Well, and set off down the hillside.

The morning was bright and sunny. The woodland tracks were smooth and dry underfoot and edged with thigh-high grasses and ferns. Streams of running water criss-crossed the woods. Mary's spirits soared. The presence of Agnes brought a powerful feeling of safety and hope. The trees themselves seemed to echo her mood, for the far hillside made a gorgeous, abundant patchwork of lush green leaves at their fullest strength, with jewelled shades of emerald, olive and beryl. She'd never realised before how stale and dank was the air in Holt Manor from the rarely-changed rushes strewn on the floors. Here in the wilderness the air was clean and smelt of sap.

Agnes went before her, a dark-green felt hat pulled firmly down over her kerchief, her skirt kilted high, easing the great strides that she took. From behind, you could not tell whether Agnes was man or woman. Mary smiled at the thought. Perhaps that was just as well.

They passed through the woods of Chancet, and headed east towards Leeshall and Buck wood, still keeping to the woodland paths. A few folk passed them with a brief nod, uninterested in the two women carrying rough bundles, too weary and harassed with their own concerns.

An old man approached with a mule piled high with coppiced wood. Agnes touched her hat to him and he nodded, but as he passed Mary he suddenly gave a growl, and snatched up her wrist. It was the silver and garnet ring on her forefinger that had caught his eye. Mary yanked hard.

'No-o-o . . .' she screamed.

He hung on tight, his face grown suddenly sly. He reached up, letting his mule go loose, and thrust back her kerchief, revealing her carefully braided hair.

Suddenly a flash of silver-grey gleamed between them. Agnes held her sharp meat knife to his throat.

The man laughed, but the laugh died in his throat as he saw the look on Agnes's face.

'Leave her be!' She spat it out.

Her face and her voice told him she'd use that knife. He threw off Mary's arm.

'Get on thy way,' Agnes snarled.

'I go . . . I go.'

His mule had set off without him, ambling along the

16

path in search of freedom. Agnes kept the knife in her hand while she watched him go running after his beast.

'That damned ring of yours,' she muttered. 'Better to have thrown it into the stream.'

Mary pulled it from her shaking fingers. ' 'Tis my mother's ring, and I'll not be parted from it.'

'At least fasten it round tha neck with twine then.'

Mary, all flustered and upset, pulled out the twine, and fixed the ring around her neck beneath her gown.

When at last they'd seen the man disappear into the far distance, Agnes sheathed her knife.

'Now we must go still faster. Get a move on, tha silly wench.'

3

The Forestwife

Mary tried walking faster to keep up with Agnes, but she found it hardgoing. Her legs ached, and the soft skin on her feet was blistered with the rubbing of the boots. Still, she knew she'd never have got this far without them, for she was not used to walking beyond her uncle's demesne.

Agnes was angry with her, that was clear; the anger seethed in every stride she took and she'd give nothing but short replies. Mary followed her with growing uncertainty. Agnes's quick action with the meat knife had saved them from being robbed, no doubt of it, but the speed and fierceness with which she'd moved had shocked Mary. This was a strange, alarming woman, unlike her fussy old nurse, and she followed her warily.

Agnes had always been different from the other servants, something of a law unto herself. She'd insisted on tramping to Loxley valley every few months to visit her brother and nephew. Somehow Owen de Holt and Dame Marjorie had accepted it, though any other servant would have been whipped. Of course they'd needed Agnes at Holt Manor, for she was also a fine herbswoman and Dame Marjorie had little skill in that way. It was well known that Agnes had saved the reeve's life, when he was

18

set upon and beaten about the head by robbers, and it was Agnes's special salves and potions that eased the aches and pains of all at the Manor House. For the first time it occurred to Mary that Agnes might be missed at Holt just as much, if not more, than her.

She broke away from her thoughts and saw with dismay that they seemed to be heading towards the thickest tangle of the wilderness. The grasses were tall and entwined with gnarled bushes and trees, and in the distance clumps of luxuriant green rushes showed the presence of marshland, and yet the path that they followed seemed firm and well trodden.

The midday sun was high in the sky when Mary saw ahead of them an ancient stone well. Agnes, who was a good way ahead, stooped to drink the water, then brought out the last of the bread from her baggage. She broke it in two, and held half of it out to Mary, who hobbled sore-footed towards the stopping place.

'And what well is this?' Mary asked, dreading the answer.

'Why, this is the Old Wife's Well, what else?'

Mary crumpled down beside the ancient carved stone trough, her baggage falling at her feet. 'Why have you brought me to this place? They say that those who pass this well are following the secret path. They go to seek the Forestwife deep in Barnsdale Forest.'

'Aye, they do say that, don't they.'

Mary rose to her feet again, angry now.

'How dare you bring me here? This is a place of evil. All decent folk who dwell in Sheaf Valley live in fear of the Forestwife. She's a witch of the worst kind. She blights the crops with curses and spells, and nobody is safe from her.'

Agnes chewed her bread, unperturbed.

' 'Tis true enough that they speak of her with fear, though I believe there's only one at Holt Manor who's

19

ever set eyes on her. Look, my girl, Barnsdale Forest is the last place they'd wish to come looking for us, and so . . .'tis straight to the Forestwife that we must go.'

'You must be mad.'

Agnes laughed, and struggled to her feet, picking up her bundle. 'Well, that is where I go. Thee must please theesen.'

'No . . . wait. Agnes! Come back!'

But Agnes strode away, following the narrower path that headed straight into the deepest darks of the dreaded forest that stretched for many miles at the heart of the wilderness.

Even though the great Roman road cut through Barnsdale Forest, everyone feared these woods and the wild bands of cut-throats who swooped out from its evil shade to prey on helpless travellers. Mary's uncle would not pass through that part of the country unless his journey was absolutely necessary, and only then if his guards were trebled and armed to the teeth.

After a moment or two of sheer, dithering panic, Mary picked up her bundle and followed Agnes, trembling with rage and fear. What else could she do? She could never find her way back by herself and Agnes, marching ahead without a backward glance, knew it.

Mary dared not let Agnes out of her sight, though she held back, refusing to walk companionably alongside her nurse. The afternoon light began to fade. Mary had passed so many trees that they merged into a scratchy green blur. Her shoulders were sore where the bundle rubbed, and her arms ached with the carrying. Every drop of that morning's joy of the woods had drained away. The forest was a cold, damp, frightening place. The tall thick trees blocked out the sun and made the barren ground beneath them smell of mould and death. Agnes, her saviour, had turned bitter and sharp.

Yes . . . she'd grown sharp. Mary brought herself to a sudden stop at the thought. Where had the vague, forgetful Agnes gone?

She forced herself to move onwards while she tried to puzzle it out. If she lost sight of Agnes now, she'd be lost indeed.

Agnes had not been her old busy efficient self for a while. Well, not at the manor anyway. Mary frowned, trying to remember.

It must have been a year since the terrible news was brought to Holt from Loxley. Agnes's brother had been found dead, out in the fields next to his plough. Robert had vanished, and he'd been named as his father's murderer. No wonder it was more than Agnes could bear.

She started to lose things and forget what she was doing. Sometimes she'd stop in the middle of speaking, as though her mind was on something else. She'd even go wandering off for a whole day at a time and come back saying nothing, not even seeming to know that she'd been gone.

Like so many odd things about Agnes, her wanderings had been tolerated. The servants whispered that the tragedy had turned her mind. No aunt could have been fonder of her nephew, that was clear for all to see, but then no sister could have been fonder of her brother, either.

Mary looked ahead through the leafy gloom, towards the small figure with its burden. Was it that same vicious Robert that she searched for now? Agnes had always claimed that Robert was innocent, but then, she would.

Now the older woman stopped where two paths met. She hesitated for a moment, but then turned decisively to the right. It was almost, Mary thought . . . almost as if she knew the paths. As if she'd been this way before.

At last Mary's anger gave way to cold and worry. She

could not stop her shoulders from shivering and her teeth from chattering. They had covered miles of forest land, and there was no possible way back. She gritted her teeth against the rubbing of her feet and strode ahead to catch up. A bad-tempered friend who led you to murderers and witches still seemed better than no friend at all in this dark and frightening place. Soon she walked just behind Agnes as before.

They were still moving as it grew dark; such a thick, black, moonless darkness as Mary had never known. She walked into branches and rocks and groaned with pain and exhaustion. At last Agnes stopped and took her arm. She spoke kindly again.

'Not far now, my honey. Not far. 'Tis a hard long way to walk, I know, but I promise thee we shall be safe.'

'By nightfall you promised.'

'I know, my lovey. I misremembered how far.'

They stumbled on, though the path was invisible. But now they walked close, arms linked, each depending on the other not to fall. At last the trees grew thin and moonlight struggled through the branches. They came to a great oak tree that stood at the entrance to a clearing edged with yew trees. The moon showed just enough for them to see a small hut. There was no light within, but a tremendous din. Chickens clucking, goats bleating, and a great squawking and fluttering of wings.

Agnes hurried forward.

'What's to do? Where is she?'

Before the oak tree stood an ancient carved stone. A smaller, wedge-shaped stone was set into the curved top. It pointed towards the cottage door. Agnes touched the stone.

'She should be here.'

Mary dropped her baggage, and looked around. Three cats ran amok amongst chickens and goats, jumping and nipping at the poor beasts' udders. Even in the dim light, it was clear that they desperately needed milking. It was not what she'd expected, this noisy domestic chaos.

Agnes pushed open the doorway and halloo'd inside the hut. There was no reply.

'Well, I don't know. I really don't.' She wandered round the side of the hovel.

Mary scooped up a small cat with white patches, just as it pounced on a screeching hen.

'Scat!' She dropped it down and clapped her hands in its face.

'Mary, come quick!' Agnes called from behind the hut. 'Fetch the candle and flint.'

Mary carried the tinderbox round to Agnes. Her hands shook as she struggled to drop a spark onto the tinder and make a flame.

'Hurry, child, hurry!'

At last she had the candle lit. She bent down towards Agnes with a sharp intake of breath.

A very old, wrinkled woman lay on the ground. She was quite still, her flesh gleamed yellow in the candlelight.

'Is she dead?' Mary whispered.

'Aye,' Agnes sighed. 'Dead at least a day and night I should say.'

'But . . . who is she?'

Agnes stood up, and Mary caught the glitter of a tear on her cheek. 'She is Selina . . . she is the Forestwife.'

'Nay,' Mary shook her head. 'She is just an old woman.'

'Just a woman,' said Agnes. 'Just a woman, like me and thee. Poor Selina, she has waited too long already. She can wait till daybreak, then we must bury her.'

They left her lying where she was, but Agnes covered her with her own cloak.

'Let's go inside and see what must be done.' She nodded towards the hut.

Mary carried the candle inside. A half sack of grain lay

in the corner, the top fastened with twine, though one clever chicken pecked at a hole in the side.

'This is what's needed,' Agnes smiled. 'We'll get no peace here till these animals are dealt with. You take up that pot and feed the hens. That's it, fill it with grain from the sack, and throw it to the poor hungry things.'

She snatched up another pot herself, and set to milking the three goats. One of the cats leapt onto her shoulder. The others made her rock on her feet, so wildly did they purr and rub against her ankles, winding their tails around the goats' legs.

'I see the way of it,' she laughed. 'I see where the milk's supposed to go.'

Mary smiled too. It was comforting to hear Agnes laugh at so ordinary a thing. Though she was puzzled by the place, she was too exhausted to do much questioning.

'I thought perhaps you came here seeking your nephew?'

Agnes looked surprised for a moment, but then answered firmly, shaking her head. 'No need to seek for Robert. He shall come looking for me.'

At last the animals were quiet, and Mary and Agnes sank down gratefully to sleep on beds of dry bracken, in the home of the Forestwife.

Bright sun shone through the open doorway, lighting the small room. Mary was comfortable and warm, the black-and-white cat curled round her feet. She yawned, then groaned as she stirred. The cat stretched and yowled, complaining that its cushion would not keep still. Never before had Mary's legs and back been so sore and unwilling to move.

Yet the homely surroundings cheered her. The room was crammed with the basic utensils for living. Pots of different sizes, hempen bags of grains, stone jars and crocks, pestle and mortar, all a little dusty and jumbled.

Great bunches of freshly-picked herbs hung from the ceiling to dry, wafting their sharp, astringent fragrance.

Another delicious smell came from a sizzling iron griddle that rested on the fire by the hearthstone. It was tended by Agnes.

'Ah ha, Sleeping Beauty has opened her eyes. There's cornmeal pancakes and cooked eggs for thee. The hens have paid thee back.'

Mary ate with relish, the feeling that all was well had returned.

'Is there water near?' she asked, thinking vaguely that she had heard the babble of a stream in the night.

'Go see for theesen,' said Agnes, and smiled.

Sleepy and bleary-eyed, Mary wandered from the hut, following the sounds. Willows drooped their branches over a small spring that bubbled up from the rocks. Mary stooped to splash her eyes, bracing herself for the chill. Her laughter rang out, so that Agnes could hear her from the cottage. She grinned hugely, knowing what the girl had found. The beautiful clear water was warm.

'This is a magical place,' Mary cried aloud to the willows, flinging the warm water into the air. 'This is a magical place that we have found.'

It was only when she returned to the cottage and Agnes pulled out a strong iron spade from behind the door, that Mary remembered with a shudder the sad, shrivelled thing behind the house.

'It must be good and deep,' Agnes insisted. She'd marked out a spot of soft earth where a golden-berried mountain ash grew close to the circling yew trees. Beyond it lay a stretch of humpy ground.

Mary groaned and rubbed her back.

'Work through it, that's how I keep my fingers moving.' Agnes flexed her rheumaticky fingers in proof. She swore that hard work was the best cure for aching legs and back.

She hovered on the edge, giving advice, for Mary had
never before dug anything, let alone a grave.

It was noon, and the sun high in the sky, before Agnes
was satisfied. She rolled Selina's body onto a woollen rug
that they'd found in the cottage, and dragged it out to the
hole. Mary was glad to leave that job to her. Then they
both lowered her gently into the pit, and Agnes pulled the
covering cloak away. Clasped between the clawlike hands
was a fine woven girdle. Agnes loosened it from the
clutching fingers and set it beside her on the ground.
Then, to Mary's disgust, she pulled out the woven rug
from beneath the frail body, and folded it carefully beside
the girdle. 'We must not waste,' she said. 'Now take up
tha shovel.'

They covered her with the warm, foresty-smelling earth.

The solemn task was almost finished when the hens set up
an anxious squawking. Mary and Agnes turned to see a
young boy carrying a smaller child. He stood in the clearing in front of the cottage, looking fearfully from the stone
pointer towards the doorway.

Agnes picked up Selina's woven girdle and the rug. She
went over to the lad while Mary finished patting down the
earth.

The boy was skinny but wiry, about ten years old. The
small girl that fretted in his arms must have been two, and
should have walked on her own, but it was clear that she
was sickly and weak, her skin red with sores.

Agnes stood before them.

'Can I help thee, lad?'

'Art thou the Forestwife?'

Though the lad spoke up firmly, his face was white and
his bare knees shook.

Agnes looked down at Selina's girdle. The intricately
woven belt lay across the palms of her hands. She hesitated for a moment, but then she dropped the rug and

cloak. Her face was solemn and pale as she fastened the girdle around her waist.

'Aye. I am the Forestwife. What is it that ails thee, child?'

4

In the Coal-digger's Hut

'My father has broken the Forest Laws.'

'Ah. Poor man.'

Agnes lifted the small girl out of the young boy's arms.

'Come, sit theesen down in the Forestwife's hut, and take some food and drink, then tha can tell us all about it. Mary, fetch them a bowl of milk, and can tha cook them both an egg?'

Mary struggled with the heavy iron griddle that was new to her, but Agnes had not let her grow up ignorant of boiling and baking and kitchen chores.

Agnes took the small girl to the spring and bathed her. The little one laughed with surprise and delight at the bubbling warm water. Then, after she'd patted her dry, Agnes gently rubbed salve from one of Selina's pots into the sore skin.

'I hope tha knows the right one,' Mary said, still fearing poisons and wicked sorcery.

'Pounded comfrey and camomile. I can tell by the smell, and so shall thee before long.'

While they ate, Agnes picked up the good rug that she'd taken from Selina's grave. She cut it into two strips, one larger than the other. Her sharp knife ripped a slit in the middle of each piece, and she slipped the soft warm wool over the head of each child, like a tunic. Then she fastened a short length of twine around each skinny belly. They both smiled at the comfort that it brought.

'A gift from Selina,' Agnes said. They giggled at that, not understanding what she meant.

'Now,' said Agnes. 'Tell us tha names, and tell us what tha can.'

'My name is Tom, and this is our little 'un, Nan. My father's a good man, but he's in trouble. He never beats us like most fathers do, and he worked right hard as a carpenter when we lived in Langden village. My father had an accident — he slipped and cut his hand with an axe. Well, he couldn't work for a while, and got no payment. He owed the Lord of Langden five days work up at the manor and couldn't do it. We had to have some meat, for my mother is big with child, and she'd been sick and worn for lack of food, just like my little sister.

'Father went out a-hunting. He wandered away to the south from where we live, and he caught us a good pair of hares with a snare, but then the Foresters of Sherwood found him with them. They claimed 'twas royal hunting land that he took them from. Father swore 'twas Barnsdale, where any man may take the beasts . . . but he couldn't prove them wrong. It's six days now, since he was sent before the Forest Justices. He came back walking all hunched and moaning.'

'Tha's done the right thing, lad, to come looking for help.' Agnes stroked his head. 'What had they done to tha father?'

The boy tried to tell, but his eyes filled with tears, and his voice choked and would not make a sound.

He spread out his right hand before them, and brought his other hand down upon it with a quick chopping action across the forefinger and thumb.

29

'Ah!' Mary caught her breath. 'His bow fingers? For a pair of hares in a snare?'

'He could not pay the fine,' said Tom.

Agnes shook her head, unsurprised. ' 'Tis all the same to them. They make sure he'll not draw bow or pull a snare again. Do not expect fair treatment in the Forest Courts.'

'But I thought King Richard freed us from the Forest Laws,' said Mary.

Agnes shook her head, smiling sadly.

'Nay, lass. He emptied the prisons when he came to the throne. They all loved him for that, but now he's stripped the country bare with his crusaders tax. The prisons are full again . . . they groan with those who'd rather break the Forest Law than starve.

'Well? Did tha father recover, child?'

Tom shook his head.

'The lord of Langden Manor came by our cottage, and we dared to hope he'd give us aid. My father's been a loyal tenant all his life. The lord spoke kind enough, and rode away, but the next morning the bailiff came knocking on our door. His lordship would not keep a carpenter who could not hold a saw. He and his men, they turned us out . . . out of our cottage and away from Langden land.'

'You poor lad,' Mary said, taking his hand. 'What then?'

'We were desperate, wandering in the forest, my father sick and all of us hungry, but we found an old coal-digger's hut and thought ourselves lucky. At least we had shelter. 'Twas last night that it all turned bad. My father began to shake and shiver and we could not rouse him. He lies in the corner, he goes like this.'

Tom showed them how his father twitched and shuddered.

'And water, like a rain shower, comes out of his skin.'

Agnes got to her feet and began sniffing and sorting amongst Selina's pots and jars.

'A festering wound,' she muttered. 'Sage to cool the
fever, then vervain and woundwort and comfrey leaves.'

'My mother,' Tom insisted. ' 'Tis my mother too. She
was right bothered by the state of my father. Then this
morning she started to moan and groan and clutch at her
belly. Well, then . . . I picked up my sister, for I dare not
leave her there, and I told my mother that I went to seek
the Forestwife.'

'Is it far?' said Agnes.

'This side of Langden village. I set off when the sun was
high in the sky, but my sister is heavy and the way was
hard to find.'

'Tha mam and dad should be proud of thee,' said Mary.
'And tha carried this lass all the way.'

Within the hour, a strange procession set off for the coal-
digger's hut. Tom led the way and Agnes followed, laden
with cloaks and ointments and bundles of dried herbs.
Mary followed leading two of the goats, steadying the
little girl astride the biggest one. As they left the clearing
Agnes stooped to swivel the pointer stone around.

It was late afternoon when they reached the hut. They
heard the screams of the frantic woman before they
reached the door. Tom ran ahead to his mother, while
Agnes dropped her bundles and followed him. Mary
found her on her knees beside the labouring woman, carefully pressing on her stomach. The poor mother groaned
bitterly and rolled her eyes.

'The child wishes to come,' said Agnes, frowning anxiously, 'but it's turned itself the wrong way round.'

'Can you do aught?' Mary winced at the woman's pain.

'I can try.'

Agnes bent over to whisper in the woman's ear.

'Take heart,' she soothed, stroking her head. 'I shall be
quick as I can.'

Then she pushed her fingers up inside the woman's body, reaching and twisting and grunting with the effort of it all. Tom's mother groaned and bit her lips, quietened by Agnes's calm assurance and faith in her own skill. The children watched in frightened silence. Then at last, with a sharp jerk that shocked the mother senseless, Agnes pulled free two kicking feet. A baby boy slithered out into the world, alive and shouting. His mother soon stirred again and blinked, then opened her eyes and set to grateful weeping at the sound of the child's cries.

Agnes turned to the sick man who groaned quietly in the corner. 'He needs me now. Can tha see to the mother and babe?' she asked Mary. 'They will be fine, now that this bairn is free.'

'But, I've never . . .'

' 'Tis naught but common sense. Get them both clean and warm and comfortable. I must look to the father.'

It was thick dark by the time Mary settled down to try to sleep, curled up beside the little girl on a thin pile of ancient straw. She sighed with exhaustion, but also with satisfaction. She'd cleared up the bloody mess of birth, and seen the new baby washed and put to the breast, all the while receiving tearful thanks from his mother, whose name was Alice.

Agnes had made herself as comfortable as she could, propped up beside the wounded man, ready to tend him through the night. She'd cleansed and dressed his wound, and spoon-fed him with her simples. Now he slept, wrapped well in the cloaks and rugs that they'd brought, still twitching at times, but breathing calmly.

By the morning his fever had gone. He was very weak, but calm and clear in his mind. Agnes milked the goats and saw the family well fed. Though there was much more that could be done, she insisted that they must return to the Forestwife's hut. The mother nodded her understanding and rose up shakily from her bed of straw to search out a small bag of dried beans. It was one of the few things they had managed to snatch as they left Langden village. She handed it to Mary.

' 'Tis all we have to pay thee with.'

Mary began to refuse. How could they take food from those who had nothing? But Agnes stepped in and took the beans.

'That pays us well enough,' she said. 'But there's something more I'd ask of thee. I've many tasks that I need a strong lad for. Will you send Tom to us, twice a week? I shall pay him with a good jug of goat's milk and a few fresh eggs.'

'Certainly he shall come,' Alice agreed. Tom looked well pleased at the plan.

Alice caught hold of Agnes by the hand, her face solemn. 'I am sad for the old wife, but glad of the new. We have great need of thee since the Sisters stopped their visiting.'

Agnes frowned. 'The sisters?'

'The Sisters of St Mary, from the convent in the woods.'

'You say they come no more?'

The woman shook her head. 'They were so good to us; to all around Langden. We wondered if we'd offended them?'

They left one of the goats behind to help the family through the first few days, with the agreement that Tom would bring it when he came to work for them.

As they wandered back through the forest, there was much on Mary's mind. Much that she wished to ask, but it was difficult to know where to start.

'Well . . . it seems that tha's taken Selina's place,' she began.

Agnes nodded, but she looked tired and sad.

'You knew her, didn't you?'

33

'Aye. I knew Selina. She helped me once, long ago. There's a great deal that you do not know about your old nurse, my lovey, and I shall tell it . . . but all in good time.'

It seemed that Mary would have to be satisfied with that for the moment, so she turned to more practical matters.

'Why did you take their beans, yet leave them with a goat? How do you know you'll ever see that beast again?'

'I took the beans in payment, which is only right . . . they have their pride. I left the goat for they need the milk, and it shows we have faith in them. We've taken upon ourselves a task that I do not think you rightly understand. Not yet.'

'What do you mean?'

Agnes fingered the woven girdle of the Forestwife. It was a beautiful thing, not like a wealthy lady's ornament, but intricately woven and rich with the forest dyes of madder, blackberry, sorrel and marigold. It was edged with finely plaited leather and fastened with a heavy metal clasp.

She sighed. 'It is an ancient and sacred pact, an agreement, between the forest folk. It will bring us safety, for none will know or even ask our names. The Forestwife may keep her mysteries. They will protect us, but there is our part of the bargain to be kept; always to be there, always to answer to those in need. It will be our refuge but, believe me, it will be hard work.'

'Do you mean that there was another Forestwife before Selina? That there's always a Forestwife?'

'Look beyond Selina's mound,' said Agnes, 'then count up the humps in the ground.'

'But . . . I have always feared the Forestwife. They call her evil and fearsome.'

Agnes laughed. 'An evil reputation has its uses. It keeps away unwelcome visitors, and those who dare to come are desperate.'

Mary remembered how poor Tom's knees had knocked when he first spoke up to the Forestwife. She wandered on in silence, thinking it all out.

At last she turned back to Agnes, grinning wickedly.

'So . . . you are the Forestwife, Agnes, and you *can* do the job, for I have always known you were a witch. But who am I? What part am I to play?'

Agnes looked thoughtful. 'That I don't know yet, my lovey, but you are most important, of that I am sure. I was not ready to leave Holt Manor, but you were. The time was right; you chose it, not me. I am quite sure there is a purpose that we cannot understand. A purpose that brought thee to these woods.'

They entered the clearing to a wild welcome from the fowls and cats and the lonesome goat. Agnes swivelled the stone around; the Forestwife was back. They laughed amidst the bleating and cackling. More of a joyful homecoming than ever Holt Manor had offered them.

They spent the rest of the day making order from the muddle that Selina's hut had become. Agnes sorted through the pots and potions, sniffing and tasting, throwing out any that were stale or sour.

Meanwhile, she sent Mary to pick great basketfuls of elder leaves and bracken tips. When she was satisfied with the amount, she set her to unpick the fur trimmings on the fine hooded purple cloak. Agnes boiled the leaves in the biggest pot and plunged the cloak into it, to pick up the woodland dyes.

When it was thoroughly drenched and dripping, they spread it out on the strong lower branches of a yew. It dripped and dribbled through the night, then dried and lightened in the midday sun. At dusk the following evening, they lifted it down all soft and warm.

Mary wrapped it around her shoulders. The soft, foresty green that the plants had given looked well with the healthy pink of her cheeks, and the dark gold of her hair.

Agnes smiled at her, hands on hips.

'You asked me yesterday what part you were to play, honey. I could not tell you then, but I know the answer now. I shall give you a new name for a new life. You are Mary de Holt no longer. I shall call you Marian. You are the beautiful green lady of the woods.'

5

The Charcoal-burner's Daughter

*A*gnes's prediction of hard work was soon proved true. From early in the morning till late at night a constant trickle of miserable folk wandered into the clearing. Many, like Tom's father, had been punished by the Forest Courts. They came trudging through the wastes and forestland from outlying villages, with scratched and blistering feet, groaning and fevered with sickening wounds. Some brought dogs with festering paws, their toes brutally crushed by the warden's men, and so made useless for hunting.

But of all the many different forms that misery took, the most common sight was a weary woman, carrying a child and followed by a trail of hungry little ones, their father thrown into gaol, the family turned from their home. Few men survived to stand trial, so dreadful were the prisons.

There was little that Agnes could do for these desperate families, but she'd serve up warm pottage, and send Tom and Marian to help them build a shelter in the woods.

There were many more suffering from the small and dreary troubles of life: the lonely, the lovesick, the hungry, the mad . . . and all their ailing animals. Each one was listened to and offered help of some sort. Only once

37

did Agnes refuse an angry, loud-mouthed woman, who sought a curse upon her mother-in-law.

'Tha must do thine own cursing,' she said. 'But best beware, for the curser may suffer the worst.'

The woman went off glowering, dragging her white-faced young son behind her.

Whenever there might have been a moment of peace or rest, Marian was sent out into the forest.

'No time to sit about, my girl. Tha must get to gathering.'

There were raspberries and bilberries, though honey was the sweetest treat. Wild thyme, rosemary, vervain and bitter rue were needed for Agnes's vital potions. Meadowsweet and lady's bedstraw flavoured their drinks and sweetened the rushes on the floor. Marian's eyes grew sharp at picking out the firm white shapes of mushrooms as she lifted the fallen leaves. Magical clumps of shaggy white fungus appeared overnight, but they must be picked and cooked before they turned black, or the taste grew foul.

Marian did as she was told, and gathered willingly enough, but she really couldn't see the need for it. Everyone paid them what they could, and they soon amassed a good store of grain. But Agnes would not touch it, swearing that it must be kept for winter.

'Well,' said Agnes watching Marian at her tasks, 'it seems my girl's thriving as never before.'

She spoke with satisfaction, but still she fretted and worried, and built up her supplies.

'I don't know what tha's bothered about.'

'Tha shall see the need . . . before next spring.'

So Marian tramped the woods with Tom as her guide, carrying baskets and bags. Her legs grew sturdy, her hands like leather, her fingers quick and strong.

Barnsdale's vast tangles and swamps were no longer frightening; they hid a network of secret paths and signs.

Marian soon discovered that the very perils of the wilderness became a source of protection to those who learned its dangers well. She grew to know each tree for miles around the clearing; to know each hovel and cottage, each warning smell and sound.

It was late in August, and a still evening when Marian returned laden with mushrooms and a few late raspberries and fat, dark bilberries.

A young girl stood hesitating by the pointer stone.

Though she had learnt to step silently, Marian purposely made a sound, not wishing to startle the girl. She was right to have done so, for the girl jumped nervously, and turned around. Marian gasped at the whiteness of her face in the gathering dusk. She knew this girl, and she knew her swollen belly.

Marian stepped forward holding out her hand, but there was no recognition in return. The girl was exhausted and ready to drop.

'Hungry?' Marian asked, offering the berries that she'd gathered. She could not keep back a wry smile, remembering the strawberries she'd once scorned.

But the amusement vanished, for the girl put out a trembling hand and sank to the floor.

Marian caught her awkwardly, shouting out to Agnes, who came running from the cottage doorway. Between them they carried her inside.

'You see who it is?' Marian cried. 'She didn't know me.'

'I see her,' said Agnes. 'I hope we can trust her.'

'What ails her, do you think? Is she having the child?'

Agnes shook her head, puzzled for once.

They settled her on the bracken-filled sacks that were their beds. As they fed her with sips of warm goat's milk, she started to revive.

She sighed, staring surprised at Agnes. 'I know thee, but I came to seek the Forestwife.'

'You have found her, honey,' Agnes laughed.

The girl stared, puzzled, for a moment, looking from one face to the other. Then her own distress came flooding back.

'I hope tha can help me, for I surely wish to die.'

They sat still on either side of her, listening to her sad story. Her name was Emma. The Ecclesall bailiff had caught her one day in the woods. He made her lie with him, threatening double land rent to her father if she told. She'd been terrified when she came to understand that she was with child. Her father had been angry, but he'd not turned her away. Then gradually, as the child had grown and moved inside her belly, she'd come to accept its presence, to wish to protect, and at last . . . almost to love. But suddenly, two days since, the child had ceased to kick or move at all. 'Then I came seeking the Forestwife, knowing my father would in truth be glad to see me and the child gone. It lies in my belly like a heavy stone. I know that it's dead, and I wish to die too.'

'No, you must not,' Marian snatched up her hand.

But Agnes shook her head. 'Let the girl rest,' she said. 'She cannot think straight after such a long hard walk in such a state. In the morning we'll talk again.'

Agnes brewed up a sleeping potion, while Marian fetched her own green cloak to cover the girl. Emma watched her wearily, with just a spark of curiosity.

'Thou art . . . the lady,' she whispered. 'Thine uncle rages over thee still . . . but I never told.'

Marian bent over her, tucking the cloak snugly around.

'Aye. I know you did not.' She gave a low laugh. 'I call myself Marian. I am the green lady now.'

Once Emma had fallen into an exhausted sleep, Agnes and Marian sat whispering together by the door.

'Can you do aught to help her?'

Agnes sighed. 'There's little I can do, for she's right,

that poor babe is quite dead inside her. All I can do is to bring it to birth. Then maybe she will recover and live — if she has the will for it.'

'She must find the will,' Marian said.

The next day was a hard one for all three.

Agnes nervously brewed up a potion from those herbs most dangerous in their uses. She fretted and fussed that the measures must be just right.

Marian sat by Emma the whole day through, helping and holding her hand. A birth took place, but a birth that lacked all joy.

In the late afternoon Marian was sent up to Selina's mound to dig a new and tiny grave. Then as the sun went down, Emma herself came walking slowly from the cottage, carrying a carefully wrapped bundle. Agnes supported her, her arms about the young girl's waist. Marian ran to take the bundle from Emma, but she shook her head.

'Let her see to it herself,' said Agnes, quite firm.

Marian backed away then, thinking Agnes hard and cruel, but as she saw the touching care with which the young girl buried her dead child, she understood that it was right.

She watched her old nurse guiding Emma through her miserable task. How was it that Agnes knew so much? For the first time the thought came to her that Agnes must herself have borne a child. Agnes had been her wet nurse, hired for her milk. She must have had a child to bring that milk. What had happened to it? Had she buried it herself like poor Emma did now? How stupid that she had never wondered before.

Marian sought around for some small token and gathered twigs of bright berries from the rowan tree. Emma took them gratefully and set them in the small hump beside Selina's mound.

The Forestwife

They both helped Emma back to bed, and Agnes brewed another sleeping drink.

Marian wandered outside, weighed down by the sadness of it all. She walked towards the strong green branches of the greatest spreading yew, and flopped down to lean against the trunk. Here in the forest she had never been so strong and free, and yet she felt that she might burst with sadness. There was hardship unlike anything she'd known.

She turned her face to the bole of the yew, sighing and wrapping her arms for comfort around its sturdy stem. As dusk crept through the forest Agnes came looking for her. She found her half asleep, still curled up there.

'Why, love, I couldn't see thee for a moment. What a sight tha makes. Has our green lady fallen in love with a tree?'

Though Marian shivered and rubbed her cheek, she could not help but smile. It was a reminder of one of the stories that Agnes used to tell when she was a child, about how a poor servant girl was lost in the woods and fell in love with a beautiful tree. The tree was really a handsome young man bewitched by a wicked old woman.

'I fear I'm not as clever a witch as that,' said Agnes, holding out her hand to pull Marian to her feet. 'And if I was, I'd turn the tree back into a fine young man for thee. Art thou sad and lonely, my lass?'

'Tha keeps me far too busy to be lonely, old witch.' Marian grinned at her.

They both went back towards the cottage.

'There's one in there that needs a friend,' said Agnes. 'I can mend her body, if fortune smiles, but . . .'

'Aye,' Marian agreed. 'I shall be her friend.'

They went inside together, glad that the day had come to its end.

Agnes was right, as usual. Emma's body mended fast, but her spirits could not. Within a few days she was up and walking easily, but she would sit for hours by the small hump of freshly turned earth beside Selina's mound. Marian worried and tried to distract her.

'Let her be,' Agnes said. 'Let her stay there as long as she wishes, however long it may take.'

When Marian had finished her chores she would go to sit with Emma. At first they sat in silence, just keeping company. Then gradually they began to talk quietly; not of the lost child, but of their early lives in Sheaf Valley, so close — yet so unlike.

Marian offered Emma the best fruits and cheese, but she'd eat little. Tom did his best to gossip and smile, even if he received nothing but a polite nod in return. Though she was clearly strong enough in body, nobody suggested that Emma might return to Ecclesall, and at least there was no more talk of wishing to die. In the end it was the charcoal-burning, and Marian's ignorance, that threw Emma into the long haul back to life.

Agnes had been worried that the small supply of charcoal in Selina's hut was almost done. In the long winter months to come, they'd have great need of slow-burning charcoal to keep the fire glowing through the nights.

Tom and Marian set to work to cut plenty of wood, and they could do that well enough. When they had a good pile ready they began to lay out a great stack in the middle of the clearing in front of the cottage.

Agnes watched, ready to call instructions from the cottage doorway, but then thought better of it, clamped her mouth shut, and went inside. Emma sat listlessly on the step, fitfully turning her head towards her baby's grave.

The stack began to grow in a wobbling, untidy way, with both builders shouting wild instructions to each other.

Emma became restless. She could not manage to sit still, and got to her feet. She firmly turned her back on them and sighed, then plodded off towards Selina's mound. But she could not quite ignore them, and turned to see again the toppling pile that grew from their hands. She could stand it no longer. Emma swung around and marched up to them, hands on hips.

'If tha builds the stack here, tha shall fill the cot with thick black smoke. And if tha sets it out like that, tha shall be burning half the clearing and the trees.'

Tom and Marian stared at her amazed. Emma licked her finger and held it up. 'The wind blows from beyond the cot. Tha must set the stack up there beside the stream. It must be built all neat and round, with a good space in the middle. I'd best show thee.'

A short while later Agnes looked out from the cottage door and smiled. All was well. There was busy building, and following of orders, and a deal of friendly chattering. The charcoal-burner's daughter was in charge.

6

The Blacksmith's Wife

Tom led his little sister, Nan, into the clearing. She was walking well now and growing strong, but Marian caught a hint of fear in the child's wide-eyed expression, and in the tense grip she kept on her brother's hand.

'Why, what ails thee little Nan?'

The child shook her head and hid her face in Tom's rump. He laughed and pushed her from him.

' 'Tis naught but the weeping in the forest that upsets her.'

Marian smiled, with a slight puzzled frown. 'And what weeping is that, Tom?'

'Has tha not heard it, lady? It often comes to me when I'm on my way to visit thee. I can't rightly say where it comes from. Some days it seems to come from all around.'

'Nay. I cannot say as I know what tha means. The forest is full of creaks and sighs, but most have a reason. 'Tis thee that's taught me so. If tha hears it again, come tell me quick, so that I can listen.'

But the strange wailing in the forest was soon forgotten, for Tom's mother, Alice, came following them through the forest to the clearing, carrying her new baby in her arms. She was out of breath with walking fast, and all upset at the news she'd heard from Langden village. Agnes and Emma appeared from inside the cottage, disturbed by the anger in her voice.

It seemed that a man who had worked the land for the manor had died of a fever, and no sooner was the man buried than the lord of Langden had turned his old demented mother from her home.

'As we know only too well,' Alice cried, 'there is no place at Langden for those who cannot work. He is a cruel master indeed. We found poor Sarah wandering in the forest three days since, half-frozen and hungry, quite out of her wits.'

Marian's eyes blazed with outrage. Agnes shook her head.

'I've known it happen before,' said Emma.

'But that is not all,' Alice insisted. 'We took Sarah into our hut and fed her, but not a word of sense could we get from her. So my husband went to Langden, as near as he dared to go. He's just come back with worse to tell.

'There is a woman who lives in Langden, she was my friend, Philippa, the blacksmith's wife. She was angry when we were turned from our home, but like them all she kept silent for fear. But she has not kept silent now. Old Sarah's treatment was too much for her. She led a gang of villagers up to the manor house and they marched into the great hall. Philippa shouted at William of Langden that Sarah should be brought back and cared for.'

Both Agnes and Emma gasped. 'What came of it?' asked Marian.

Alice bit at her lip. 'She is clapped into a scold's bridle, and fastened to the stocks. William of Langden has sent to the Sheriff to have her declared outlaw. They will brand her and chase her from Langden land.'

'Branded? Do you mean they'll burn her?' Marian demanded.

'Aye. Burn her with the outlaw's mark. 'Twill be there on her forehead for all to see.'

'What of the other villagers? What of her husband? '

'They say he sits and weeps in his forge. If he complains, he'll lose his living. Who shall feed their children then?'

They stood together in silence, their faces pale and tight. Only Marian could not keep still; she paced up and down clenching her fists.

'Come settle down, my lovey,' Agnes begged. ' 'Tis a harsh thing indeed to treat this poor woman so. But we must know when there is naught to be done.'

Suddenly Marian stopped her pacing.

'Nay, Agnes, there is something we may try. We cannot stop her being outlawed, but she shall not be branded. We must get her away from Langden tonight.'

Marian, Emma, Tom and his mother set out for the village as soon as dusk fell.

Agnes walked with them just to the edge of the clearing, Alice's baby in her arms, for the Forestwife must stay behind. She caught at Marian's arm, her face drawn with worry.

'Must tha do this, lovey? We can be safe here in the heart of Barnsdale. Must tha go looking for trouble?'

For a moment they all hesitated, frightened of what they planned.

'I cannot leave Philippa to be burned and shamed,' said Alice. 'She was ever my good friend, but you owe her naught.'

' 'Tis not for your Philippa, that I go,' said Marian. ' 'Tis for thee and thy man, and young Tom here. 'Tis for all the ills this lord of Langden did thee.'

'Bless you,' whispered Alice.

Agnes sighed, but she reached up to kiss Marian.

47

'Tha's a fierce rash little lass, but maybe I begin to see what part tha plays.'

Marian hugged her. 'We'll be back before tha knows.'

They moved off quietly, into the forest night.

Tom and Alice knew the way so well that the journey was not difficult. They moved stealthily, their cloaks wrapped close for warmth and disguise. Marian's fingers kept fastening around the handle of the sharp meat knife that she'd stuck into her belt; checking and touching, and wondering if she could use it should the need arise.

At last they came in sight of the stocks, set on the village common. The surrounding huts were quiet.

The blacksmith's wife stood tall and upright, her shape a dark shadow in the moonlight. She was unguarded, for who in that place would dare to rescue her? Marian looked up at that still figure. The heavy metal bridle stuck out around her head, ugly and humiliating. How could she stand so straight up there, alone and cold, yet refusing to sit or droop? A strong woman indeed. She began to understand why Alice cared so.

A bubble of hot anger burst over Marian, her doubts and fears fled. 'Look at that foul bridle,' she hissed to Emma. 'How can we get it off her?'

Emma shook her head hopelessly. 'Only they will have the key.'

'There is but one man who can cut it off,' said Alice. 'That man is her husband.'

'Will he risk it?' asked Emma.

'He'd better,' said Marian.

Tom was sent to the forge to warn the blacksmith and make sure that all was ready.

'Right,' said Marian gripping tightly onto the handle of her knife. 'Let us get her now.'

Once they had made their move they went fast, creeping swiftly towards the stocks.

'Hush Phil, 'tis Alice.' Tom's mother murmured low, so that Philippa would not be afraid, and know she was with friends.

Marian quickly cut through the rope that fastened the woman to the stocks, then, supporting her on either side, they made their way to the forge.

The blacksmith had candles lit, ready to set to work with his smallest knives and files.

It was clear the job could not be done instantly. Alice made Philippa sit. She stroked her hands and spoke soothing words. The blacksmith was smaller than his wife, but his muscles braided his arms like corded rope. He worked hard and fast, choking and weeping all the time. Emma kept a look-out by the outer door.

Marian lifted a curtain at the back of the forge. Six children slept soundly in pallets round a glowing fire. Philippa had much to leave.

'There's a barking dog, and light up on the common,' Emma cried out, before the work was done.

'No time left,' said Marian.

The blacksmith gave a powerful great rasp with his file, Philippa groaned and the metal snapped open. She was white-faced and staring as they lifted the burden from her head, and pulled the metal thong gently from her mouth. Dark blood trickled from her lips and fresh blood ran down her cheek. The last sharp effort had gashed her face.

Alice pulled her to her feet, and they were off, their cloaks whirling through the door.

'Do not leave me with this,' the blacksmith cried, picking up the hated bridle.

'I'll take it, sir,' said Tom.

'Phil . . . ippa!' the blacksmith's cry followed them out, into the cold dark night.

There was running and shouting and blazing torches

coming closer as they headed for the forest. Several of the villagers saw them go, but the captain and his armed guards were bravely pointed in the wrong direction. The village was finding its courage once again.

They set off running through the forest, and at first all went well, but soon concern for Philippa slowed them down. She was a tall, well-built woman, but as they moved further from Langden and her ordeal, the stubborn pride that had kept her going began to drain away fast. She shivered and shook and made strange sounds.

' 'Tis all we can expect,' Alice cried out, frantic for her friend. 'Those wicked bridles mash the tongue. We must get her to the Forestwife.'

The last mile was a hard struggle, and they almost carried Philippa between them, but at last they reached the clearing and the blacksmith's wife was given into Agnes's tender care.

All through the next day Philippa was nursed and tended. She was carefully spoon-fed, but slept heavily and made no sound. Alice watched her anxiously, and whispered her fears to Marian.

'I've known a scold's bridle so hurt the tongue that they never speak clear again.'

Marian had her own doubts. After the first wild pleasure in their success, she'd grown miserable at the sadness of Philippa's situation. The sleeping children by the fireside kept creeping into her mind.

Early that evening Philippa stirred and opened her eyes. She held her hand out to Alice, but stared with surprise at the tiny hut crowded with women. Tom squeezed in through the doorway, sensing that something was happening, followed by one of the goats and a clucking hen.

'We've little to welcome thee with,' said Marian. 'We

took thee from the stocks to save thee from branding. I fear we've scarred tha face instead.'

Philippa put her fingertips to the cut, feeling gently and wincing, but then she pulled herself upwards until she sat. Much to their surprise, she would not rest with that, she pushed away Alice's supporting hand, and struggled to her feet. Then she stood tall and straight, as they'd seen her by the stocks, but now her eyes burned bright with triumph.

She moved her mouth awkwardly, as though chewing.

They all held their breath.

Then slowly but clearly she spoke. 'We have defied the manor.'

Tom raised both his arms and clapped and cheered. The goats and chickens squawked and bleated in reply, and the hut was filled with laughter and uproar.

The blacksmith's wife did not return to her bed, not that day nor any day. She took a quick look around the clearing and told Agnes that the Forestwife was in need of more shelter. Everyone was quick to agree, and the following days were full of cutting and sawing and hammering. Tom's father came to give his advice, though he could not do much of the work. It was Philippa who did the heavy lifting and sawing, throwing herself into it with relish, speaking steadily and with good humour, though slowly.

Alice came through the woods every day, to give help and see her friend. She brought old Sarah with her, who wandered round the clearing happy as a child and got in everyone's way. Once the alarm was raised when Alice noticed that the old woman was missing and work had to be stopped while they searched and brought her back.

Marian blinked back tears when she saw Philippa quietly stroke the cheek of Alice's baby, or stoop to pat little Nan's head.

Gradually a lean-to grew on the side of the hut, making

twice as much room as before. It was sturdily built and smelt of fresh oak, so that those who slept beneath the Forestwife's roof slept safe and warm and dry.

7

The Green Man

*I*t was an early evening in late September, with a cool wind blowing through the yew trees, when Marian heard the wailing once more.

The clearing was quiet, for Philippa had gone to take Sarah back to the coal-digger's hut, saying she'd stay with Alice for the night. They had found the old woman wandering, lost in the forest again. Poor Sarah had been quite distressed.

'The trees are crying,' she insisted. 'They lose their leaves and they moan and weep.'

The others had smiled kindly, but Marian had set to wondering, remembering the wailing that Tom and little Nan had heard.

Agnes and Emma were busy in the new lean-to, crumbling dried herbs into pots to keep for winter use, when Marian thought that she could hear crying herself. She said nothing, but wandered out into the clearing, holding up her licked fingertip as Emma did. The wind could carry sounds a long way, she'd learnt that much.

She wandered towards her favourite tree, the great yew. She stood for a moment beneath its sweeping branches, fingering the small pink fruit and breathing in the clean scent of resin.

It was only as she turned to go, glancing down to where a bramble caught her foot, that she saw it. Her stomach leapt — a hand, sticking out from beneath the curling bracken. The skin was the same gingery brown as the dried bracken fronds, making it hard to see. Her heart thumped and her throat went tight as she bent down and carefully pulled away the leaves. Close by the yew, well hidden amongst the undergrowth, a man lay fast asleep.

He was young and thin-cheeked, with a dark growth of beard. He was dressed in a grey hog-skin jerkin, worn silver in patches like the yew tree's bark, and dark ginger leggings that blended with the colour of his hand and the drying bracken. His cloak was a deep foresty green, like her own. Marian stared down at him, then up into the branches of the yew, her mind drifting into a dream of the green lady and her forest lover. It seemed he was part of the woodland itself; grown from the trees, the bracken and the rich dark earth. He was a very beautiful young man.

Suddenly he groaned in his sleep and muttered, twitching restlessly. She bent close, wrinkling her nose at the rank smell of sweat and sickness, and saw that his face was bruised. His cloak was good homespun, but ragged and torn. How stupid she'd been. This was no fairy lover. He was not asleep, but ill. The skin on his cheeks was white beneath smudged dirt and glistened with moisture. He was real enough — he stank — and he was somehow familiar. Yes . . . her hands shook at the thought. She knew him; she had seen him once before, though only from a distance, when he'd stayed with Maud and Harry at the mill. He was Agnes's nephew, Robert, the fierce wolfshead, the wicked one.

He cried out, a low, growling sound like a wounded boar.

'Mother,' he seemed to cry, then he rolled to the side. His hand and stomach were caked in dried blood.

Marian turned and ran, shouting for Agnes.

'Why, what is it, lass?' Agnes came to the doorway, a bunch of lavender in her hand.

'Agnes. He is here beneath the great tree. It is Robert. He is hurt, and he cries out for . . . his mother?'

'Show me,' Agnes dropped the flowers and ran.

She bent down beneath the branches, then fell to her knees beside the lad. She touched his head, and caught hold of his hand.

'Mother,' the beastlike growl came again.

Agnes looked up into Marian's puzzled face. 'He has found his mother,' she said. 'For Robert is not my nephew, he is my son.'

Marian stared open-mouthed, but Robert groaned again and Agnes turned quickly back to him.

'No time to stand there gaping, girl. Take up his legs, while I lift him round the shoulders. Ah, he's no weight! What has the lad been doing these months?'

They carried him carefully into the cottage and settled him on the bedding. Emma came forward to help, supposing him just another unfortunate lad who'd come seeking the Forestwife.

There was dark dried blood on his hand and shirt. Agnes pulled open his jerkin, clicking her tongue at all the clotting blood. Then she turned his head to the side, tenderly feeling at the temples. He had a black eye and yellow and grey bruising above.

Agnes clicked her tongue again.

'Clout on the head, and a sword cut. Marian! Fetch water! Quick, lass!'

Marian picked up the bucket and ran.

She dipped the bucket into the clean warm water as quickly as she could, though her hands would not stop shaking. Then she set to frowning as Agnes's words sank in.

'What has he been doing, these months?' As far as she knew, Agnes had not seen Robert for a year at least, and what had she called him? Her son?

Marian shook her head, she could not understand at all, but there was not time to stop and think.

When she returned, Agnes and Emma knelt over Robert, their heads bent together, carefully cutting away the shreds of bloodsoaked homespun from his shirt that had dried around the wound. Emma glanced anxiously across at Agnes, then down at Robert. Something had been said between them . . . Emma knew.

Without waiting to be told, Marian squeezed out a cloth in clean warm water and began the job of washing him. Robert still muttered and rolled his head, the words making no sense, his mind still far away. She bent over him, gently cleaning the dust and mud from his face. There was broken skin beneath his matted hair. She wrinkled her nostrils as she wiped dried vomit from his cheek. What a fool she had been! How ever could she have thought him so beautiful . . . the magical green man?

Despite the offers of help that came, Agnes insisted on sitting up all night with the wounded lad, and in the morning her devotion was rewarded. Robert was calm and quiet, smiling up at his mother with recognition. Marian carried in a bowl of bread soaked in fresh warm goat's milk. She knelt at his side. He smiled at her and whispered his thanks, then turned to his mother.

'Where is the fancy m'lady then?'

Marian froze, and Agnes pressed her lips tight together.

Robert looked from one to the other, his mouth falling open.

'She is not the one?' He laughed low and winced. 'My lady of Holt, with a freckled nose and dirty face?'

'I would clout thee good and hard,' said Agnes, 'if someone had not already done it for me.'

Marian's hands started to shake, so that the milk looked like to spill. 'I am Marian,' she said. 'I am Mary de Holt no longer.'

Robert said nothing, he would not look at her, but smirked down at his feet. Marian was clearly beneath his contempt, though she could not see why.

'Give me the bowl,' said Agnes, taking it from her. 'Take no notice, my lovey, he knows nowt, and believe me, when this head of his is mended he will think a different way.'

She spoke sharply over Robert's head, trying to catch Marian's eye, and make her smile.

But Marian could not. She knelt there for a moment, staring down at the trodden earth floor, her fists clenched, fighting to hold back tears. Then suddenly she leapt to her feet and ran outside into the cold clean air. She hated this sick man, with his sneering mouth, hated the very smell of him. And besides all this, was he not a murderer?

She strode across the clearing, taking her usual path to the great yew, but as she lifted her hands to its soft, sweeping branches she stopped, remembering how she had found him there. She turned away, her anger stronger than ever. He had somehow defiled the beautiful tree. She could never turn to it again without thinking of him.

Then, as she shifted, she caught another movement from the corner of her eye. She whipped her head round quickly, catching only the sense of a dark shadow slipping away, and the faint crackle of dry leaves. Branches of the further, smaller yew trembled, but when she caught hold of them, there was nothing there. They were thick, sturdy boughs, and the wind had dropped.

Agnes came from the cottage, calling her name. Marian did not move. She thought of hiding, punishing her.

Her old nurse saw her standing amongst the yews and

called again. Marian still would not turn towards her, but she waited, her face turned away. She stood there while Agnes came to take her hand.

'Tha must let me explain it all to thee, lovey. You owe me that. I left him with my brother when he were less than two years old. I left him when I went to be your nurse.'

'Aye.' Marian sighed. 'I suppose I can but hear thee out.'

Agnes led her back to the hut, but turned her away from the old room where Robert lay. They went and sat together in the new lean-to. Marian paused at the door, glancing quickly round the clearing.

'I thought I saw someone just now out there, hiding amongst the trees. I thought I heard a voice.'

Agnes joined her, but there was no sound or movement.

'Maybe you did see something,' she whispered. 'There's others, and they'll come for him.'

Agnes settled herself in the corner, by the pots of herbs. Instinctively she took up the work she'd dropped in haste the night before, crumbling dried comfrey leaves into pots. Marian picked a bunch of crisp, dark-golden tansy flowers, and joined her in the task.

'His father,' she began, nodding her head towards the old room, 'his father, my husband, was Adam Fitzooth, a yeoman farmer and a freeman. We had a bit of land over Wakefield way, that we rented from the Lord of Oldcotes, for payment and fieldwork at ploughing and harvest.'

'What?' said Marian, staring in surprise. 'I cannot see thee as a married woman.'

Agnes laughed. 'Well I was, and for many a year. I was happy with him too, though we wished for children, and they never came.'

'But?'

'Don't rush me, girl, I must tell it my way. We had a good life together . . . but then it all went wrong. It was

the year of the great rebellion. The northern lords cut
themselves off from King Henry, and there was a great call
to arms. Adam was the best bowman in the county, he
went to fight for the King. The Lord of Oldcotes sent him
in his place, and promised us gold and gifts. But Adam
didn't go for what he'd earn, he went to fight for the
King — the fool.'

'You didn't want him to go?'

'No. King Henry cared naught for England, and his son
is even worse. 'Twas yet another stupid quarrel, amongst
those you'd think had power enough. I could not care
who won or lost. But Adam would not listen to me, and
well . . . he went . . . and there's not a lot more to tell.
He was killed, and when we got the news the Lord of
Oldcotes turned me from our land. I was with child you
see, and not young. It was clear I couldn't do the work
that was owed. I'd had my wish for a child come true, but
it came too late.'

Marian dropped the herbs, and took Agnes's hands in
her own. 'All these years, I've known so little. What
became of you?'

'I found Selina, that's what became of me. I wandered
miserable, hungry and sick for days, no . . . for weeks,
but at last I walked into this clearing. I'd heard wild tales
of the Forestwife, but I was desperate, much like poor
Emma. Selina took me in.'

Marian sat silently, listening with growing sadness.

Agnes smiled, though she blinked back tears.

'I was luckier than Emma, for my babe was born alive
and strong. We lived here with Selina for more than a
year. Perhaps we should have stayed, but . . . perhaps
what happened was meant to be.' She squeezed Marian's
arm.

'My brother lived in Loxley valley, and worked a small
piece of land. I was strong again and wished to show him
my son; so I went to find him. He made us both welcome,

and begged us to stay. It was when we were there that we heard from Maud and Harry of tha mother's death, and how the lord of Holt needed a wet nurse for his sister's child. I thought to offer myself.

'But what of Robert?'

'He was almost two years old and he was strong, and ready to be weaned. A wet nurse earns as good a wage as any woman can hope for. I only meant to stay with thee for a year or so. I told them that my child had died. That's what they wanted to hear. They wouldn't want a nurse as might have put her own bairn first. My brother loved Robert and swore that he'd care for him as though he were his own. He kept his word, right to the end. I left them together, as well set up as any father and son. I thought I could save a bit of money and then go back to them.'

'Well? What happened? Why did tha stay so long?'

Agnes shrugged her shoulders and sighed. 'I could not leave thee, when the time came.'

Marian smiled. 'Was I such a sweet child then?'

'Nay. Tha were a poor, thin, grumpy little thing. 'Twas only I that loved thee. I could not leave thee to Dame Marjorie's tender care.'

'Huh.' Marian twisted a lock of her hair between her fingers, then tugged at it. 'So . . . he is angry that you stayed with me?'

Agnes frowned. 'Yes, he is, though he knows well enough that I loved him. How often did I go walking over the hills to be with him. I took him food and clothing, the best Holt Manor had. And when my brother was killed and Robert blamed, he came to hide in Beauchief Woods.'

'But . . . ?'

'No. He did not kill my brother, though there's many a wild and stupid thing he has done. They were truly like father and son, and they had been quarrelling. Their neighbours knew it, and it looked bad for Robert. But he loved my brother, and could not have killed him.'

'Even in rage?'

'No. He could not,' Agnes snapped. 'So he hid in the woods, and Maud's and Harry's son brought me messages. Where do you think I wandered off to all those times? I knew they all thought my wits were fading, up at Holt Manor. I let them think it. Meanwhile I took him food and clothes and all he needed.'

Marian's mouth dropped open. 'So when I ran away, and you followed me, he was left alone?'

'Nay, nay. He'd been gone a while then. He had heard that the Sheriff was arming Nottingham Castle, and not too fussy who he took so long as they could draw a bow and not run from a fight. He's a fine archer, Robert, just like his father, and ripe with anger. He craved a fight, so off he went, taking Harry's and Maud's son with him.'

'Do you mean Muchlyn, the small one?'

'Aye. He were always daft with Robert. Would do aught he told him. Maud and Harry were wild with worry, and I was vexed with him, but neither lad would listen, and they went.'

'How is he hurt then?'

Agnes shook her head. 'I've not got it quite clear yet, but there has been trouble amongst the men-at-arms. He's like his father, is Robert, in his passionate support for the King, and naught I can say will make him see sense. He found out that the Sheriff was really arming the castle for Count John, against the return of Richard. It's ended in a quarrel, and they had to fight their way out and run . . . right through Sherwood Forest he's come.'

They sat in silence for a moment, Marian finding it hard to take in all she had heard.

Agnes sighed. 'So that is what he is like, my lovey. Do not take what he says to heart. Though he's my son, he is a wild and reckless lad. I fear for him.'

8

Muchlyn and John

*L*aughter and shouted greetings could be heard out in the clearing. Philippa was returning with Tom, and it sounded as though Alice and her husband were with them.

Agnes got to her feet, and rolled up her sleeves ready to return to her work. 'Now tha knows the truth, lovey. Right or wrong, 'tis what happened, and cannot be undone. Can tha try to understand his ignorant way?'

Marian frowned and nodded. 'Aye, maybe I can.'

There was a great deal of noise and chatter and explaining to be done. None of the other women was surprised that Agnes should have a son, and Robert was clucked and fussed over to his heart's content.

He said no more to Marian — indeed, he ignored her — and she kept out of his way, quietly getting on with the dreary chores, fetching the water, gathering wood, and feeding the animals.

Two days passed, and Robert looked much better. He still winced and groaned when he moved or twisted; but his colour returned, and he did much chattering with Emma and Philippa. He told them tales of the short time he'd spent in the Sheriff's pay; the mischief he and his friends had revelled in, and the chaos they'd caused. Emma listened shyly, smiling and hesitant. Philippa pinched his cheeks and slapped his leg. She said he was a grand lad, for the Sheriff of Nottinghamshire was known even in Langden for his meanness and cruelty.

Once Marian carried a pitcher of water into the hut when they were talking. She felt a sudden hush as she entered, and noticed the tailing off of Philippa's voice. '. . . without her I'd have been branded, you see.'

There was an awkward silence as Marian poured the water into a bowl. Then, as she turned, Philippa spoke up with her usual openness. 'We've been telling Robert how you stole me away from Langden stocks.'

Robert grinned shamefaced, and looked away.

'Oh . . . have you now,' said Marian, and went outside as quickly as she could.

It was on the third day that Marian again had the feeling that they were being watched. The same low murmur of voices, and slipping away of shadows amongst the trees. She went about her tasks as usual, ignoring her suspicions, but when the first glooms of evening fell, she set off as though leaving the clearing, wrapped in her green cloak and hood. She hadn't gone far before she turned round, kicked off her boots, and tucked them under her arm.

She had learned to move through the forest like a lithe green ghost, treading soundlessly through the undergrowth, her long dark cloak echoing the shapes and shades of the woodland. Stealthily she returned to the clearing, moving towards the great yew. Such a tree offered shelter from wind and rain, and a soft matting of dried leaves beneath.

There they were, just where she thought they'd be, a big man with wide shoulders, sitting with his back against the trunk of the yew, and a smaller man hunched beside him on the ground. Marian smiled, she thought she knew the small man . . . and she certainly had no fear of him.

Closer she moved, and closer still; then silently sat down between them.

The big man leapt to his feet, light and quick as a wild cat. He whipped a knife from his belt.

'Nay,' she screamed, terrified by her stupidity. 'I know thee. 'Tis Robert of Loxley tha seeks. I've news of him.'

'What news?' The big man caught her round the back of the neck, his great height lifting her from her feet, his breath stale in her face. The sharp blade of the knife pressed against her throat.

'He is there in the cottage, with his mother. And I know you,' she grabbed at the small man's kirtle. 'You are from Holt Cornmill. They call you Muchlyn, Maud and Harry's son.'

'Aye . . . tha knows me right enough,' his voice faltered with surprise, 'but who art thou? Leave her be, John, and let her speak.' Muchlyn pushed back the steady clenched hand that held the knife at her throat.

'I am Marian, I live with the Forestwife.'

'Th'art . . . the lady. John . . . she is the one, the one that ran away from Holt.'

John laughed and set her on her feet again. He sheathed his knife. 'Tha'art a fool, m'lady, to creep up so on John of Hathersage — but tha's a fearless fool, I'll say that for thee.'

Marian breathed out and rubbed her throat, trying to snatch back a bit of dignity. 'I came to say . . . to tell thee both, that there's shelter and food in the cottage of the Forestwife.'

The two men followed her out of the undergrowth, and warily went with her to the cottage door. The big man towered above her, but Marian could see when the candle-

light caught his face that he was nothing but a great,
strong, overgrown lad. As soon as they saw Robert looking well and comfortable, they set their suspicions aside.

'We lost thee, Rob,' cried Muchlyn. 'We saw thee jump
from the steps, and we took our chance to run, while they
followed thee. We knew tha'd seek the Forestwife — if tha
lived.'

Both lads had suffered a battering and bruising in the
fight that had ended their service with the Sheriff of
Nottinghamshire. Muchlyn limped and groaned as he set
his foot to the ground. Agnes was soon mashing a comfrey poultice and wrapping up his leg.

'Why, lad, how has tha managed to walk so far on that?'

Muchlyn laughed, and thumped the big man's thigh. 'I
had a great ox to carry me. I call him Little'un for he's so
tall. He calls me Big'un.'

John laughed and thumped him back, making Much's
eyes water, so that they all had to smile and shake their
heads.

Robert struggled to his feet, though he winced with the
pain. He made play of grabbing John by the neck, grinning into his face.

'Want some fight, big man . . . pick on me.'

'Be still,' said Agnes, 'or I cannot mend this lad's
leg . . . sparring like young wolves.' She clicked her
tongue.

Marian backed away, crouching in the shadowy corner.

'Tha'd best show Rob what else I carried,' said John, his
face bright with excitement. 'I swore and blasted at him
that he was so heavy for such a little 'un. Show him,
Much.'

Muchlyn's eyes shone, and his dirty face cracked into a
great grin. Slowly, from inside his kirtle he drew out a
glinting silver cup, and then a platter, and then another
cup, and more plates, all wrought in the finest chastened
silver.

The whole company drew breath as each piece was revealed.

Robert put out his hand to touch and take one cup. He gave a cruel laugh. Marian shivered at the sound of it.

'Now Much, tha's made theesen into a thief. Tha's wolf indeed. Wolfshead now, the same as me.'

'Aye.' Muchlyn grinned, pleased at that.

Agnes found ale that she'd brewed from a gift of grain, and there was gossip and laughing and storytelling till late into the night.

They stayed in the Forestwife's clearing for two days. Robert was on his feet and walking well, and Much hobbled nimbly, supported on a stick that John shaped into a crutch. At first they were busy cutting great staves for longbows from the straightest branches of the yews, and ash staves for their arrows. They gathered up the feathers from the hens and geese, shouting with pleasure at the fine fletchings they'd make.

But on the second day they gathered by the doorstep, cuffing each other and sparring restlessly and getting in the way. They ate as though they thought they'd never see another meal, shouting foul oaths at each other all the while, hopeless and uncomfortable at the sight of the miserable procession of those who sought the Forestwife.

Tom hovered around them, listening to their yarns, copying their oaths, refusing his work, and leaving Marian to do the chores. John would follow Emma in her round of tasks, attempting to help her stack the wood that she tirelessly replaced when each slow charcoal burning was done. He did not tease her or touch her, but it was plain to see that she shrank away from him.

Agnes watched them all anxiously, rubbing her stiff fingers, and shaking her head and clicking her tongue. Suddenly it was clear that they could not go on as they were.

Agnes caught hold of Philippa's arm. ' 'Tis no good,' she said. 'We must be rid of them.'

'Aye.'

Philippa firmly took John aside, and Agnes called Robert into the lean-to.

Marian watched from the cottage doorway as Philippa wagged her head and folded her arms, speaking solemnly to John. She could not hear what was said, but the big lad listened well, his face serious. Philippa pointed to the tiny grave beside Selina's.

Then Agnes called Marian inside. Mother and son sat close together, Robert looking none too pleased. 'These lads are on their way,' said Agnes. 'They are well enough to fend for themselves. Well enough to be looking to cause trouble here.'

Marian said nothing, though she was glad enough to hear it.

Agnes got up, and Robert awkwardly followed her.

'Come here, both.'

Agnes stood between them, taking each one by the hand. She spoke slowly and seriously. 'You two are the ones that I love best in all the world. T'would be a blessing on me, if you could manage to agree.'

They stood in silence for a moment, Robert and Marian both red-faced and staring at the ground.

'Well?'

'Aye,' they both muttered and nodded their heads. Then, very stiff and formal, Robert bowed to Marian, and just as stiffly she dropped a curtsy to him.

All the women gathered to see them go.

'Where will you be heading?' asked Agnes, anxious again.

'South,' said Robert. 'South, to where the great road passes through the forests. Full of rich travellers it is, yet close to Sherwood bounds, so that we may not starve for lack of venison.'

'Aye,' said John. 'We shall do well enough there for a while.'

Agnes sighed. 'I do not wish to nurse thee for a severed hand, or hear tha's died in Nottingham gaol.'

Robert hugged her and laughed.

'They'd have to catch us first, Mother. We are too fast and fine for them. And we have other plans that might find us a shelter and food for the winter.'

'Oh aye, and where might that shelter be?'

'We think of going north to Howden Manor, for we hear the Bishop of Durham is gathering fighting men there. Old though he is, he's loyal to Richard still, and he's making ready to take Tickhill Castle from Count John.'

'Can tha find naught to do but fight, lads?' Philippa shook her head.

'Nay,' they laughed. 'What else is there for such as us?'

John bowed to Agnes. 'I thank thee for our rest and food. We will not linger here, for you have strange sad ghosts that cry and moan about your forest. Isn't that right, Much?'

'Aye. John fears nowt, but he got the shivers when he heard the weeping that's carried in the wind. It came to us beneath the branches of your great yew.'

With much waving and calling the three lads went on their way, but Marian turned away from the others as they saw them off. She went back into the clearing, heading straight towards the tallest tree, her eyes sharp for every movement, listening for the slightest sound.

❀❀❀❀❀❀❀❀❀❀❀❀❀

9
The Heretics

❀❀❀❀❀❀❀❀❀❀❀❀❀

*T*he clearing seemed strangely quiet after Robert and his friends had gone, though Marian had little time to notice it. The autumn gathering was in full swing, and Agnes fretted about her stocks more than ever.

Marian and Emma tramped the woods with Tom, seeking out blackberries and crab apples for pasties and pies, elderberries for wine, and hips and haws for Agnes's remedies. Then for the winter stocks they must gather and store chestnuts, hazel nuts, beech mast and acorns.

Marian and Tom stood beneath the yew tree in the dusk, though they were weary from their hard day's work.

'I can't hear it,' said Tom. 'Anyways . . . it don't come every night.'

Marian put her finger to her lips to silence him. She was determined that once and for all she would hear the weeping in the woods.

They stood there still and listening, though there was nothing but an owl hooting, and the distant rustling that always came from the wind in the trees and the running of small animals.

Tom sighed. 'We could stand here till dawn and still not hear it.'

'You go then,' Marian snapped. 'I'll see to it myself.'

Tom shrugged his shoulders and turned towards the cottage as though he might well take her at her word, but as he bent down to pick up their heavy baskets . . . it came. Just a faint eerie sound, so indistinct that it could have been imagined. Tom stopped and turned to Marian.

'You heard it too?' she whispered.

He nodded. 'I think I did.'

They both stood in silence, until once more the faint cry reached them.

'Wolves?'

Tom shook his head. 'I've heard wolves afore.'

Marian nodded. 'There . . . it comes from beyond the stream, that way. Will you come with me, Tom?'

'Aye.'

It was hard to follow at first, for the cries came in faltering, fitful bursts. Sometimes they'd miss them for the crack of a twig, or mistake them for a wild cat's howl.

At last, as the glooms of evening thickened around them, the cries became louder and more distinct.

Tom stopped and scratched his head. 'We go towards Langden village. I swear this is the way.'

The cry came again, and Tom turned his head. 'No . . . not Langden. Over there, towards . . .'

'Where?' cried Marian. 'What is it?'

Tom suddenly ran ahead in the direction of the sounds. Marian chased after him, and caught him by the arm. He stopped and turned to her, frowning.

'This is close to where the Sisters live.'

'You mean . . . the convent? The Sisters who have vanished from the woods?'

'Aye.'

Once he'd got the convent in his mind, Tom went fast,

Marian striding along beside him. There was no doubt
about it, the crying came from that direction. The night
grew darker and the miserable wailing loud and fearful.
Tom reached the top of a grassy bank and stopped. They
looked down the hillside to where the trees had been
cleared for the small convent buildings and kitchen
gardens. A strongly built wooden fence protected it all. A
low light showed at one end of the building. To Marian it
all looked peaceful and organised. The gentle clucking of
fowls and the grunt of pigs rose from the sheds.

'What is it, Tom? It seems to me that all is well.'

Tom shook his head. 'The Sisters never built that great
stockade. 'Twas open for all to come and go.'

Suddenly the sobbing came again, not from the convent, but from further up the ravine, where the sloping
hillside was wooded. Cries of such despair that they
flooded the valley with sadness. A shiver ran down Marian's spine, lifting the hairs on her neck.

Tom clutched her hand and trembled, pointing up the
valley.

' 'Tis the Seeress,' he whispered.

As Marian turned off towards the source of such misery,
hoofbeats rang out below. A rider was fast heading in the
same direction. Marian grabbed Tom's hand and pulled
him after her. They stumbled down the hillside as quickly
as they could in the dark.

Then came the harsh shouting of a man's voice, and
loud banging.

Marian ran fast, but she could not see clearly what was
ahead. It looked to her almost as if the man on horseback
attacked a tiny chicken hut. There was the clatter of wood
on wood, and angry bellowing, then the clang of metal,
and more shouting. The wailing ceased and the horseman
whirled around, his horse braying loud in protest. He
headed back towards the convent at a good speed. Marian

crouched with Tom behind the gorse scrub, as he galloped past.

The crying had ceased, but in its place there came a small pathetic whimpering that Marian found even more distressing. It seemed to come from the chicken hut.

Marian got up to approach it, but Tom held her back.

'No,' he whispered, more scared than ever. ' 'Tis her. 'Tis the Seeress.'

'But who is she? Have they locked her in there?'

'No,' Tom shook his head frantically. 'Don't you understand? She has locked herself in there. She is not like the other nuns. She never comes out.'

'Ah,' said Marian. 'An anchorite. I have heard of such women, but never —'

'I have not seen her,' Tom interrupted, 'but I know all about her. She is strange and frightening, some say she is mad — more of a witch than the . . . the . . .'

Marian smiled. 'More of a witch than the Forestwife?'

She could not see his face clearly, but she knew that Tom smiled back at her.

'Aye. But then the Forestwife is just . . . Agnes.'

'Yes, said Marian. 'This Seeress is but a woman too. And though I cannot see why, someone is treating her very ill.'

Tom followed her then, though he was still fearful. They crept down towards the dark hump of the hut, half buried in earth. A stale smell of decay seemed to emanate from the tiny dwelling, and hover in the damp shrouding mists that surrounded it. There came again the sound of low whimpering, and the rustle of long robes.

There was silence, and then a shaky, frightened voice. 'Who is't?'

'I am Marian. I live with the Forestwife and help her.'

There was silence for a moment and then another shuffle. A patch of white moved, indistinct in the darkness of a small window, barred from the outside and covered with a fine metal mesh. The quavering voice came again.

'Then I saw true. Selina's dead.'

'Aye, I fear she is, but I have come to see what ails thee. Why does tha weep and wail so? We have heard thee from afar.'

'I weep because I must. I give utterance to their misery. They weep in silence, so I must cry out for them.'

The voice rose in a wild passion. Tom clutched tight to Marian's sleeve.

'Men of God they call themselves, but 'tis no god of mine that starves little children of the sun. And so you see, I must weep. I weep for myself and them.'

Marian sighed. It was hard to understand what it all meant, and the thought came that maybe Tom had been right when he spoke of madness.

But it was Tom himself who answered now.

'She is the Seeress.' He spoke with conviction. 'What she sees is the truth.'

Marian shook her head. 'But . . .'

'You never knew 'em,' he insisted, nodding back over his shoulder towards the convent. 'Something is wrong down there. The Sisters lived there, quiet-like and good, but they were busy as bees in a hive, digging their gardens, scrubbing and cleaning and tending the beasts. They came to our village twice a week with food and medicines. They brewed a good ale. And — and Mother Veronica, she was fat, and she laughed, and she brought the two little lasses with her. Naught but bairns they were, carrying their own small baskets.'

Marian frowned, but the Seeress spoke calmly. 'The lad speaks truth. He understands.'

'Who was that man,' Marian asked, 'and has he hurt thee?'

'Nay.' The Seeress answered now with quiet strength. 'He bangs on this grille and shouts to shut me up. But I shall not be silenced. He is one of the white monks, Cistercians from the great abbey. You see, we are Cistercian nuns, and by right they may rule us, but though we've been here fifteen years, they have never interested themselves in us. Then three months since, six of them came, and with them the Lay Brothers.'

Marian and Tom listened as she told them in quiet, sensible tones, how the Lay Brothers had built a stockade around the convent. Then the monks insisted that the nuns be locked up in their cells, even the two children. There they were to spend their time in prayer, and contemplate their wickedness. Dreadful rumours of heresy had reached the Abbot. Nuns had no business to go wandering about all over the countryside, as they had done, meddling in things that did not concern them. Worst of all, they'd allowed their lazy chaplain, Brother James, to roam the forest with his dog, while they — the nuns — took their own services, preached their own sermons, held their chapters and meetings without the advice of a priest.

Tom listened wide-eyed and open-mouthed.

'Why, 'tis true enough, they did all that, but they brought comfort to our village, and life has been hard since they've gone.'

The Seeress went on speaking, clear and firm.

'The Lay Brothers have returned to the abbey, but the white monks stay. That one you saw, he brings a little bread and water each day. I see no other but Brother James. He wanders about the woods with his dog in a miserable drunken state, but he is still my friend. The Sisters and even the little girls, they weep within their cells.'

'But how . . . ?'

Tom's pressure on her arm answered. 'Ah yes. The Seeress knows.'

'I chose this life,' she went on. 'It was a hard life, but not miserable. The Sisters consulted me, they brought me their worries and their joys. Sister Catherine looked after me well. These monks,' she shuddered, 'they will not even bring me water to . . . cleanse myself.' Her voice shook.

Marian could bear no more.

'I can bring thee water. I could fetch it from the stream, if I had something to carry it in.'

The Seeress was eager. 'I have a wooden bucket, and I would be glad of help.'

There came the squeak of a rusting bolt, and then a sudden clap of wood on wood. A small hatch flopped open beside the window grille. A pair of startlingly white hands held out a bucket. Marian wrinkled her nose at the smell that issued through the opening.

'Do not look at me,' the Seeress cried. 'I am banished from the world. None may see my face.'

Though Marian wished very much to peer inside, she kept her glance down. She could not bear to be the cause of more distress.

She filled the bucket from the stream, and handed it carefully back.

'We will come again,' she promised, 'and though I cannot think how, I swear that you shall have help. We have friends who once lived at Langden. They will stand by you, and the Sisters.'

'Aye, that we will,' said Tom.

Marian stood up to go, but through the darkness she saw the faint, thin shape of a hand come stretching and beseeching through a small space at the bottom of the grille. Marian clasped it in her own, though it was damp from the water, and carried with it a sour smell. She could have wept to feel the frail bones beneath the cold white skin.

The Seeress clung to her for a moment, then she

whispered, 'My heart leaps up to find such a friend. You shall bring us all joy, I see that clear enough.'

They set off back through the forest. Both Tom and Marian were quiet and shaken by what they'd found. It was when they reached the top of the hill above the convent that Tom almost fell over a dark shape, curled up in a dip. A growl and flash of white teeth warned them to step backwards fast. Then a man's deep voice fell to cursing, and there came the strong smell of ale.

'Watch out. 'Tis him.' Tom pulled Marian away. 'All right, all right, boy,' he soothed. 'No harm, no harm.'

'What was that?' Marian whispered, once they seemed far enough away. She'd been glad enough to do as Tom had told her.

'That were the one she spoke of. That were Brother James. He's a big fat fellow and he likes his ale, though he's kind enough when sober. That hound of his never leaves his side. Once it belonged to the lord of Langden. 'Twas his best hunting dog, but it was found in Sherwood by the regarders and they lamed it.'

'Poor thing, no wonder it growls and snarls.'

'Well, that is their right. But they hadn't realised who it belonged to. There was trouble, and William of Langden went into one of his rages. He swore he'd cut the beast's throat now that it was useless for hunting.'

'I don't like the sound of that man,' said Marian. 'The more I hear of him, the more I dread him. Well, how did that drunken monk get the dog?'

'He marched into the great hall at Langden Manor, red-faced and full of ale, and asked for it. First the lord said no, but the monk lifted up his great staff and said he'd fight any man William chose, to get the dog.'

'So did he fight?'

'Nay. Brother James is a big strong feller. William of Langden kicked the dog, and said he might have the useless cur, if he was so bothered about it. Though he's nasty and mean, he wouldn't want to lose one of his best fighting men, not for a dog.'

'So Brother James took it?'

'Aye. And though it's not much of a hunter, it defends its new master as you saw, and it's learnt a trick or two that might surprise its old master.'

Marian walked on deep in thought, then she turned again to Tom.

'You say he's kind enough when sober, this Brother James. Did he care for the nuns do you think?'

Tom laughed. 'Aye, he cared for them. Specially Mother Veronica.'

'I shall have to go seek him, in the daylight. Though I think I might take Philippa along.'

10

The Sisters of St Mary

Marian was surprised, for Philippa hesitated when she asked her to go looking for Brother James.

'I never thought tha'd have a doubt. Not for a moment. I cannot bear to leave them there so miserable and imprisoned.'

Agnes pushed her down onto the stool, and set a bowl of steaming porridge in her lap.

'Calm theesen. Tha's fair done in, tramping through the forest all night, and me worrying and wondering what tha's up to. We cannot go rushing into this, there's much to think about. The Sisters chose to make their vows. That's no light matter, and disobedience in the Church may be called heresy.'

Emma caught her breath. 'You mean, they could — '

'Aye,' Agnes was stern. 'They could burn, by right of the Church's law, should they disobey the Abbot.'

Philippa sighed. 'Agnes is right. 'Tis not the law of the manor, or even the law of the King. This is a matter for the Church and maybe even for the Pope. More powerful than the King, he is. I will not turn my back on it, Marian. I owe the Sisters much, and I will come with thee, but we must tread carefully.

78

'And there is something else, that I . . .' Philippa's voice trailed off, so unlike her usual firm way of speaking.

They all looked up at her.

'It is this. That we must go close by Langden, and I . . . well, I have been thinking lately that I must go back. Not to stay. I know that cannot be, but . . . it comes into my mind that William of Langden may treat my little ones ill, to punish me. So you see . . .'

There was quiet for a moment, then Emma spoke.

'I'll go with thee to Langden. Tha must be certain that the little 'uns are safe.'

'Let us all three go,' said Marian, 'and we may meet the drunken monk upon our way.'

The three women set off, well wrapped and Marian with her meat knife in her belt. Tom ran at their heels like a hound, he would not be left at home, and they were soon glad of him, for none of them knew the woods as well as he.

Brother James was not difficult to find, for they saw his great dog resting, but still alert, beside an ivy-covered fallen tree. The monk snored loudly, in a pile of beech leaves, sheltered in the bowl of earth that the torn-up roots had left. Beside him was a pile of chicken bones, a fallen stoneware flagon by his feet.

The dog leapt up, growling at their approach, but the monk snored on.

They moved forward warily.

'Brother James, Brother James . . . shift theesen,' Marian called, pulling her knife from her belt.

The dog crouched, preparing to spring.

'Wake up, tha great fat fool,' Philippa bellowed.

'What? What?' Brother James, snorted and jumped to his feet. The dog snarled and leapt at Marian, a flying shadow of black fur. She screamed with fright and staggered backwards, angry and shocked.

'Pax, Snap!' the monk shouted.

Though Marian was shaken, she realised that she was unharmed. The knife had gone from her hand; it glinted from the corner of the dog's mouth, as he dropped down onto his haunches, obedient and watchful now.

Brother James blinked round at them, fuddled and muzzy in the morning sun.

The dog growled again, and dropped the knife. His master stared and rubbed his eyes, puzzled by what he saw. Three women, steadfastly placing themselves to surround him. There was the crack of a twig behind, and he turned to see a young lad.

Two of the women were only girls, one frightened but determined, the other red-faced and angry at the loss of her knife. The third, who stood before him, was big and strong, and he knew her well, just as he knew the lad.

'Peace, Snap,' he soothed the dog again.

He staggered forward, holding out his hand to Philippa.

'What the devil . . . ? Haul me out of this hole.'

He laughed as she heaved him up.

'Tha's not lost thy strong arm nor thine impudence, since tha became a wicked outlaw woman. I wondered what had become of thee.'

'From what we've been hearing, tha's become a bit of an outlaw theesen.' Philippa grinned. 'But 'tis Mother Veronica and the Sisters that we're fearful for.'

Brother James sat down amongst them, rubbing at his dirty stubbly chin and pulling his mud-stained habit straight. What he told them proved the Seeress true. He swore that he'd been threatened with expulsion from the Church. The monks had turned him out of the convent, into the woods, as punishment for neglecting his work and allowing the nuns the freedom they'd enjoyed. He'd had it in mind to go off to the Abbot and plead for them, but not much faith in the reception that he'd get. He couldn't quite bring himself to desert the Sisters with whom he'd lived so comfortably. Since then, he'd hung around the stockade, stealing ale and food whenever he got the chance.

He wept as he spoke, and heaved great sighs. Emma listened with sympathy, but Marian and Philippa fidgeted and shook their heads.

'So tha can get inside the convent, when tha wants?' Philippa demanded.

He grinned then. 'I know that building better than those prating monks. I creep inside while they chant their offices. They don't even know I've been or what I've taken. I carried a sup of ale to the Seeress, but she'll do naught but whine and wail.'

' 'Tis her cries that have told us that there's trouble,' Marian snapped, exasperated by him. 'You could have let the Sisters out. You must know where to find the keys. You could have done something for them!'

He stared up at her, puzzled at her rage. Who was this furious young girl in a good green cloak?

He turned to Philippa for some sense. 'I could maybe let them out, but where would they go? They're vowed to obedience. Dear God! 'Tis heresy indeed that tha suggests.'

Philippa sighed. ' 'Tis their wishes that we need to understand. Instead of filching ale, can tha not search out Mother Veronica and offer her our help?'

He scratched his head, where stubble grew on the old tonsured patch. 'I can try. Aye, I can do that.'

'If they wish it,' said Marian, 'we shall help them build some shelter in the forest. There are more of us . . . friends that we may call to aid us.'

He scrambled to his feet, clicking his fingers to Snap, who leapt at once to his command.

'Mother Veronica always did things her own way. I shall do what you ask, young woman. No need to look so

fierce at me. Tha may take tha knife back from Snap. I
shall meet thee here tomorrow at dusk.'

'Aye, we've other errands.' Philippa was restless to be
off to Langden.

Marian took her knife back, still frowning, but as they
walked away, she turned to see Brother James filling the
flagon with water from the stream. She could not help
but smile as he poured it over his head, snorting and
shuddering, while the great black shadow beside him
danced and barked.

Emma and Marian approached the blacksmith's cottage by
the forge, leaving Philippa hidden in the gorse scrub at the
edge of the woods. It was a quiet midmorning, most of the
village folk busy at their chores. The blacksmith recog-
nised Marian, and welcomed them inside. As they stood
by the warm fire's glow and looked around the small neat
home, they could see that all was well. The children were
strong, and all had good warm clothes and clean faces.

'Tha's been looking after them well,' said Marian,
impressed and pleased for Philippa's sake.

'Aye, but I've had help,' her husband told them, though
there was something of a puzzle in his face.

'From thy neighbours?'

'My neighbours have been grand, that's true. But we
have had better help than they could have given.'

'What then?'

He shrugged his shoulders. 'Presents. Presents of good
food and clothing, brought in secret in the night.'

'And you do not know who sends them?' Marian's eyes
were wide with interest.

The blacksmith shook his head. 'No one in Langden
could give such presents. No one but the lord.'

He laughed, though there was no joy in the sound.

'We can be sure it is not him. The only one we can think

of is his wife, the Lady Matilda, but she is a poor sick woman, rarely seen. Some say that William beats her.'

'Why should he do that?' Marian demanded.

'She's given him but one daughter. William wants a son as his heir. There are many who would say that that is reason enough.'

Marian shook her head at the injustice of it all.

'She's a kindly woman though,' the blacksmith spoke softly, 'and I swear these presents come from her.'

The children were wild with excitement at the thought of seeing their mother, and yet they fell obediently quiet when they were told. Used to living in fear, thought Marian.

Emma took three of the children straight off with her to see their mother, each carrying log baskets, as though they were going to search out firewood. Marian waited until they returned and then gathered up the others, insisting that there must be no fuss or commotion.

'Will tha come too and bring the bairn?' she asked the blacksmith.

He hesitated and turned towards the forge. 'I have much work in hand . . .' His voice trailed off, and Marian frowned.

'I daresay Philippa will wish to see you too.'

The man sighed, then turned back to her.

'Aye, surely I shall come, and bring the bairn, but I fear it will not please Philippa.'

The man took the smallest boy from the crib where he slept, and wrapped him well in a warm, soft woven blanket, one of the mysterious gifts. Then he set off with Marian and the two other children.

Philippa rushed forward to hug her children, but then she moved slowly towards her husband and suddenly slapped his face sharply. Marian flinched and backed away from them; the blacksmith had been right.

'That is for this scar.' Philippa touched the long red

weal that still showed on her cheek, flaming livid with her anger. Then suddenly her face changed. She flung her arms around the man and child, hugging them both and planting a kiss upon her husband's mouth.

'That is for keeping my little 'uns so well. Now give me that bairn.'

She gathered the baby into her arms and settled back against a tree stump, rocking the child, her cheek against his head.

'Rowlie, my little Rowland,' she crooned.

Marian smiled with relief, but saw that the man still looked troubled.

Philippa's smile faded. Slowly the rocking stopped; she looked down at her child, then up at her husband.

'How long have I been gone from Langden?'

He sighed and sat down beside her, putting out his strong, work-marked hand to touch the baby's head. ' 'Tis all but six weeks, my love.'

Philippa's voice shook. 'And this bairn has not grown a jot.' She unwrapped the small body. 'His little arms and legs are like sticks.'

The blacksmith shook his head. 'I swear that I have done my best, and others have tried too, but we cannot get him to feed. He should be trying his feet by now, but he frets and will not take milk or sops.'

Philippa's face crumpled. 'Mother's milk is what he needs, and I have none for him.'

Marian sat down beside them, understanding their concern now. The two older children stood still and quiet, watching.

'We have good fresh goats' milk in the clearing,' Marian spoke gently. 'And the Forestwife to give advice. Best of all, we have his mam.'

'Aye,' Philippa picked up the idea and smiled. 'I shall take him back with me.'

'I think it's maybe best,' her husband agreed.

'Will William of Langden see that he's gone?' Marian asked.

The blacksmith laughed. 'Do you think he knows or cares how many children we have? And no one else will point it out to him.'

'Does he treat you ill because of me?' Philippa asked.

He shook his head. 'He needs his horses shod, and his guards well armed.'

Once the decision was made, Philippa was keen to be on her way, and get the baby back to Agnes. One of the other children was sent to tell Emma, and to fetch the good wrappings and baby clothes that had appeared with the other gifts.

Goodbyes were said, and soon Philippa was striding smiling through the forest with her little lad strapped to her front. Marian and Emma struggled to keep up with her. Emma had gone very quiet.

They were close to the clearing when Philippa slowed her pace at last. She had begun to see and understand Emma's silent pain. She stopped by the pointer stone and caught hold of her hand.

'I never thought,' she said. 'Seeing me with this little 'un must hurt thee sore.'

Emma's eyes filled with tears, but she lifted her hand and gently stroked the fine hair on Rowland's head.

'Your Rowlie is a sweet child,' she whispered.

'He is that, and I must try my best to save him. I'll never do it on my own. I'll need a deal of help.'

'Aye,' said Emma shyly. 'I'd be glad to do what I can.'

'Might tha take him in for me, while I sort out these wrappings?'

'May I?' Emma held out her arms, her chin trembling.

Agnes came to greet them, surprised to see Marian and Tom carrying rugs and blankets, Philippa grinning and satisfied, and Emma with a baby in her arms.

11

Bunches of Rosemary

*A*gnes examined the small child carefully, pressing gently on his legs and arms, and at last lifting him up to try his feet. Philippa and Emma both watched anxiously. At first the two poor, thin legs trailed, and the child stared blankly into Agnes's face, but then he drew up his knees and kicked his feet down weakly.

'Boo!' Agnes shouted suddenly.

The child jumped in her arms, and then, slowly, a delightful one-toothed smile brightened his face.

'There's naught wrong with this little chap,' Agnes turned to Philippa. 'Naught wrong that good goats' milk, fresh air and mother's love won't cure.'

Philippa snatched up her child, laughing with relief, and Emma went to fetch a cup of milk, still warm from the beast.

All the next day Philippa fussed and fretted over little Rowland, and Emma ran round in circles, fetching and carrying for the child.

Late in the afternoon Marian brought out her cloak, and fastened on her boots. Philippa stared at her, puzzled, for a moment, then suddenly got to her feet, the child crying out at the sharp movement.

'Brother James! I forgot.'

Marian laughed.

'Settle theesen down again. I shall take Tom with me. I do not need thee, nor Emma. There's nothing to fear from him, I know that now.'

Brother James was waiting as he'd promised, leaning against a sturdy oak, Snap sitting quietly beside him. The monk lumbered to his feet at their approach.

'Well?' Marian demanded at once. 'What of the Sisters? Has tha spoken with them?'

He bowed deeply, chuckling and ignoring her questions. 'Greetings to you, my wild lady of the woods.'

Marian sighed with impatience and Tom grinned at the monk. Then Brother James's face grew solemn. 'Indeed, I've news for you. Mother Veronica and the Sisters are longing for the freedom of the woods. I can let them out. Can you build shelter for them?'

Marian's face lit up. 'We shall do our very best.'

'We'll do that all right,' Tom agreed.

'Can they really burn for this?' Marian asked, suddenly frightened by the plan.

The fat monk's cheeks trembled. 'By right and by the Church's law they could. But then they would have to be hunted and discovered, and carried off for judgement. These bishops are too busy fighting amongst themselves. I hear that Geoffrey of York has excommunicated Hugh of Durham yet again, and even sent his men to smash Hugh's altars. Still the old man laughs in his face, and gathers his army about him. In truth, I cannot see even the most vindictive churchman paying men to search these vast and desolate wastes for six poor old women and two dowerless girls.

' 'Tis the two lasses, Anna and Margaret, that are the

greatest worry for Veronica. They were given into her care as babes. Unmarriageable daughters! Young Margaret's face is scarred by the hare lip, and Anna born with a crooked back. How can Veronica set such children outside the Church's law?'

'But should they then spend their lives like prisoners, locked away in cells?' Marian insisted.

'Nay,' he shook his head. 'And that is why she will bring them with her. You know these Sisters set themselves up as working nuns. They never claimed to lead the solitary life of contemplation . . . only the Seeress aspires to that. Oh no, Veronica and the Sisters never wished to be saints, just decent women leading safe and useful lives. That's why they were so happy with their special saint.'

'What? The Blessed Virgin?'

'Nay!' He laughed. 'They are the Sisters of St Mary Magdalen.'

As Marian turned to go, Tom caught her arm.

'Will the Sisters bring their beasts?'

Marian looked surprised.

'Oh yes, they must bring their beasts.' Brother James agreed. 'How should they get through the winter without them?'

Brother James paused and sighed. 'There's one who'll not come. The Seeress will never leave her cell. I spoke with her last night, and though I talked till dawn, I could not win her over. All she cares is that the nuns go free. She will not break her vow.'

Marian remembered the childlike hand in hers. 'We'll see. I'll speak to her.'

Brother James shrugged his shoulders. He touched her head. 'A heretic's blessing,' he whispered.

Marian stood quietly with Tom, watching him stride purposefully away through the crackling leaves, Snap bounding after with his awkward gait.

It took many days and a great deal of help searching through miles of forest, wild wastes and marshes, before a site for the new forest convent was found. It had to be far from Langden Manor and the old convent, but it had to have a good supply of strong straight timber for building and, most important of all, clean running water that would not fail.

At last such a site was found, far south towards Sherwood, yet still within the thickest tangle of Barnsdale. A marsh lay to the north-eastern side. Dangerous marshland would offer protection. They chose a patch of level ground, sheltered by a sloping bank of beech and holly trees.

Philippa sent Tom to Langden to beg axes and saws from her husband. Tom's father, his damaged hand healing well, went around the chosen clearing, marking the trees to be felled.

Tom returned with a great sack of tools, but the blacksmith regretted that he was short of nails, and could not spare the few he'd got.

'Of course he's short, for 'twas me that made his nails,' said Philippa. 'If only I had iron to melt down, I could make all the nails we need and more for him.'

Tom looked at her and bit his lip. 'I know where there's iron,' he said. 'But I fear tha might not like it, Philippa.'

'What can tha mean?'

Tom ran to the side of the clearing and dived into one of the smaller yews, where thick green branches swept the ground. There was a clanking sound, then he emerged, his forehead wrinkled with worry, dragging the rusting scold's bridle by the chain.

Philippa's face fell. The busy work and chatter around them ceased.

Tom stopped, dismayed. 'I feared tha'd not like it. I carried it that night, and I knew how tha must sicken at the sight of it, so I hid it. Shall I drag it away and you'll see it no more?'

Philippa stared white-faced at him. For a moment she seemed unable to answer, but then she spoke up, her voice stern.

'Nay. Bring it to me.'

He dragged it on, till it rolled clattering before her feet. She suddenly laughed, and bent to kiss him.

'Tha's a good lad. 'Twill make a thousand nails, and I shall beat it and hammer it and thrust it into the fire.'

She fetched the stout sweeping brush that stood at the cottage door, and whacked the hated thing across the grass. Everyone clapped and cheered to see her treat it so.

Later that afternoon, Marian set off alone, laden with freshly-picked bunches of rosemary. As darkness came, a bright moon sailed above the leaflorn branches of the trees. She clambered down the bank near the convent of St Mary, heading for the lonely cell of the Seeress.

The woodlands were quiet and still, though the air was damp and chilly. Moonshine threw graceful waving shadows across the ground, creating constantly changing patterns of dark and light. Marian moved slowly towards the hump of earth that covered the small cell, with a growing sense of intrusion. A low clicking came from the hut, and, as she moved closer, Marian realised that the sounds came from the Seeress. She stood still for a moment, recalling those desperate cries that had brought her here before. These sounds, strange though they were, held no misery.

Marian saw a startling and lovely sight. A young dog fox sat by the Seeress's grille, twitching his ears and making small growling yaps in response to the eerie clicking song. Marian froze, mouth open, scarcely breathing. The magic held only for a moment. Some other sense told of her presence. The creature turned towards her, and in that instant she glimpsed the deep yellow fire that burned in his eyes. Then he was off, leaping into the undergrowth, leaving only the rank smell of fox to tell of his presence there.

The Seeress caught her breath, and Marian hastily stepped forward to explain.

' 'Tis I, Marian, the Forestwife's girl.'

The Seeress's voice was calm. 'I knew 'twas not one of the monks. They have left me much alone of late. I weep no longer, now that Brother James has told me of thy plans.'

'Aye. We make a hiding place in the forest. I swear we shall do all we can to keep the Sisters safe. But you must come too. The Brothers are bound to be angry. They may harm you, or even leave you to starve.'

'I stay here,' she insisted. There was no waver in her voice.

'But why?' Marian was almost angry.

'I made my vow, and I keep it. I am not like the others. Mother Veronica and Catherine were always decent, religious women. I am here for my sin.'

Marian sighed. 'What sin? Whatever could you be guilty of that demands this of you?'

The white face shimmered behind the grille and vanished.

'Do not go!' Marian pleaded.

Once more the indistinct, white, moonlike oval moved towards the grille, and the childlike hand came creeping through the space beneath. Marian caught it up, frightened by its coldness, rubbing it between her own warm palms.

'It was a great sin,' the Seeress's voice shook. 'Nobody knows . . . only my brother, and one other. 'Twas my brother built this place for me, and sent me here. I must bear this life with patience, and hope for salvation through my suffering.'

Marian let go the hand. She raked her fingers through her hair in frustration. What could she say? What could she do to shake this blind belief?

Then the Seeress spoke again, her voice warm and loving.

'I am not unhappy. I have great faith in you. I cannot always see, as they think I can, and I cannot see clear what lies ahead, but this I know . . . in your presence, I feel that there is hope for us all. There is even hope for me.'

Marian sighed. 'I almost forgot. I have brought thee a good supply of the cleansing herb, rosemary. At least you may keep your cell all clean and sweet.'

'You see,' the Seeress's voice was deep with pleasure, 'tha knows full well what I desire most. Brother James brings me ale, but he would never think of rosemary.'

Marian did not stay till dawn as Brother James had done. She returned to the Forestwife's cottage before the candles had guttered for the night. There was no hope of changing the Seeress's mind. Marian was sure of it, and must content herself with promises that she should be watched and cared for, even when the other nuns were gone.

Over the next few days, those who'd pledged themselves to help were thrown into a wild fury of work and preparation.

Marian rushed about shouting and begging and worrying. She was all in a spin with excitement and fear at what they were daring to do. Philippa's skills and strong arms were much in demand. She strode through the clearing with her little lad strapped to her chest. Whenever she had a dangerous job to do, Emma stood by with willing arms, ready to cuddle and fuss him. Despite the hard work that surrounded him, the child was clearly thriving. Tom insisted that they change his name from Rowland to Rowan, for the fine red cheeks that he'd gained.

The frame of a small building was raised with strong

beechwood planks and Philippa's good nails. Everyone was needed to slap wet mud onto the wattle panels, woven about with moss and twigs. There were no thatching materials close by, so great bundles of rushes and heather were dragged through the forest tracks. The clearing that they'd created soon became known as the Magdalen Assart. Even the smallest children worked till the wintery sun sank behind the hill.

12

The Magdalen Assart

All too soon, the appointed evening came when Brother James would free the Sisters. Marian, Alice, Philippa and Emma crept up to the hill above the convent. Brother James was waiting there with Tom and Snap.

'Is the potion ready?' he asked. He was sweating and anxious, his fat cheeks shook with concern.

'Aye.' Marian took a small phial from her belt. ' 'Twas not easy to persuade her though. Agnes swears that they will sleep till midday, though the taste may be bitter.'

'I shall see it goes in the richest dark red wine.'

Brother James held Marian's hand for just a moment.

'I pray we do right, my bold lady.'

Then he set off through the thickening twilight, faithful Snap limping at his heels.

The four women and Tom settled down to wait. There'd been others willing to come, but they feared large numbers might draw attention and spoil the plan. In the end it came back to just the four.

All was quiet in the convent buildings beneath the hill. They waited, tense and strained, barely whispering.

The chapel bell rang for the end of vespers, and the monks filed out. There were quickening footsteps below

94

them as the Brothers moved in line to the refectory. Candles flickered through the small windows, and the faint chink of cups and platters could be heard. The meal began.

Up on the hillside Marian and her friends grew hungry and anxious. The darkness gathered around them.

'What now?' whispered Emma. 'How will we know?'

'We must listen for the compline bell,' said Marian. 'If it rings, we have failed to drug them, and must wait till they go to their beds.'

'But how will we know when compline time comes?'

Marian frowned. 'Brother James will give us some sign.'

Never had time dragged so. A bright moon drifted from the clouds and lit the woodland hillside so that they shrank into the bushes, worried that they'd be seen.

The lights still glimmered in the refectory, but it seemed the distant sounds of chatter had ceased. Still there was no bell.

'The time for their praying must be past,' said Emma.

'I doubt they take their prayers so seriously,' said Philippa. 'They break what other rules they wish.'

Marian stood up. 'I think we should go down, but quiet and careful, mind.'

'Aye.' They all agreed. They'd waited long enough.

All stealthily and slow, they crept down the bank towards the convent. Still there was no sound nor sign of movement from inside. Then as they gathered at the bottom of the hill a man's voice suddenly rose, chanting the prayers of the night.

They all stood frozen together, listening and scared.

The singing did not come from the chapel. All at once the lone voice was answered by a chorus of female voices, some deep and sweet, some childlike in their tones. The nuns were singing compline with Brother James.

Relief spread from Marian to the others. They smiled at

each other, though they stood with itching feet beside the door, wishing to be on their way.

At last the singing stopped, and suddenly there was wild bustle and chaos. The door was flung open and six nuns poured out, each loaded with bags and sacks so that they could scarcely move.

'Do the brothers sleep?' Marian asked.

'They snore like pigs, my darling,' said a fat nun, her arms wrapped tightly around two frightened little girls.

'Sister Catherine is henwife,' said Brother James. 'Go with her and catch the fowls.'

'I have bags for them,' said Emma, rushing off after the flustered nun.

'I'm pigwife,' said a tall young nun. 'Sister Rosamund. Who'll help me with the swine?'

'You go, Tom,' said Brother James, 'and Snap. Go fetch the pigs!'

Marian reeled amongst the turmoil, wondering where to help next. A nervous young nun clutched the arm of one who was old and stooped.

'Sister Christina, she cannot walk well,' she cried.

'We'll make a chair with our arms and carry her,' said Marian, snatching up the young nun's hands, and bending down to pick the old woman bodily from the ground.

Then all at once they were off, in a noisy, bustling gang. Pushing and shoving and tripping over each other's feet, they went off into the chilly forest night. Soon the pushing stopped and turned to puffing, as women and animals set themselves to climb the hill.

'Ooh dear, you should leave me, such a nuisance I am!' Sister Christina trembled and cried.

'Hush now,' said Marian. 'You're no weight at all.' And that was true enough, for the old nun was frail and light.

Mother Veronica went ahead with the two little girls, talking calmly to them all the while.

'What an adventure, my darlings.'

As they reached the top of the hill, Sister Christina continued to whittle and whine so that Marian was tempted to take her at her word and leave her there, but she caught the eye of the young nun who helped her with the carrying, and they both giggled instead. Sister Christina looked suspiciously from one to the other and fell silent.

Once they had gained the top of the hill they felt that they could slow down a little, and make some sort of order. Emma and the henwife were the last to reach the top. They set the others smiling, for they both carried angry squawking hens in bags, and more tucked beneath each arm. The cockerel rode precariously upon the old nun's head, flapping his clipped wings and crowing frantically.

They moved on through the forest, vowing their thanks to Agnes's potion, for they made enough noise to wake the dead. It was slow progress, for one way and another they had to keep stopping. The hens squawked and complained, and fluttered away whenever they got the chance. The pigs were puzzled that they could not root and snuffle wherever fine acorns could be found. Snap earned his keep, and more, by chasing runaways and fetching them back with gentle nips. Sister Christina began her whimpering once again, till Mother Veronica said she wished they'd left her behind, making the two pale children giggle.

With all the fuss and stopping, it was almost dawn as they neared the Magdalen clearing. They were joined and greeted along the way by forest folk, for the nuns were widely known for their kindness. By the time they reached the assart, faint gleams of morning light came through the stark branches of the beech trees. The carrying was shared about, and all the nuns walked free of their burdens.

'Why, child,' Sister Catherine put up a wrinkled hand to touch Marian's cheek, 'I feel I know thee, now I see thy face clear in the light.'

Marian shook her head and smiled at the old nun's vagueness. She looked around for Tom, but could not see him. She wondered where he was, but could not go hunting for him. He knew the woods better than any, she told herself. As they reached the top of the wooded slope and looked down upon the clearing, a quietness fell. Marian lowered Sister Christina gently to her feet. There was a moment of anxiety amongst the forest folk. The hut they'd raised was rough and small compared to the sturdy convent buildings.

'Someone has made us a fire,' said Mother Veronica.

Smoke trickled out of a hole in the roof. Agnes appeared at the open doorway with mugs of ale on a long wooden platter. Little Rowan staggered out behind her, clutching at her skirt. Two black-and-white kittens jumped at his wobbling ankles — they'd been brought to keep the building clear of mice.

The two novices left Mother Veronica's side and crept towards the kittens, laughing with delight and clicking their fingers.

Mother Veronica took hold of Brother James's hand. She turned to Marian, smiling. 'This is a blessed spot you've brought us to. I thank you with all my heart.'

It was late next evening when Tom came running up to the newly-built convent hut.

'They rage,' he cried, laughing and excited. 'They rage and curse and run round in circles. Never have you heard such oaths.'

'Do you mean the monks?' Marian asked.

'Aye. I crept back to the convent, and I sat with the Seeress till morning. Then I hid amongst the bushes, high up on the hill.'

'What happened?'

'Agnes's potion worked true. There was no sight nor sound of them till the sun was high. Then they came stumbling from the great hall, angry and white-faced and bleary-eyed, rubbing their heads and groaning.'

'Have they harmed the Seeress?'

'Nay. I think they've forgotten her in their anger. They blunder around the building, still searching for hidden nuns and food. All they can find is a sack of oatmeal and plenty of drink. The last I saw they set to broaching a cask to quench their fury. I guess they'll sleep again.'

The next few days were spent helping the Sisters to settle into their new home. Although the oldest nun was frail, Marian saw that the others were strong and capable, and used to working together. Sister Catherine was old but spry, she soon had a gang of willing workers building winter shelter for her hens.

Sister Rosamund had been the cellaress, but she'd declined to bring away the stocks of wine and ale. Instead she'd brought sacks of grain, beans and peas. Good stocks for the coming winter, Marian pointed out to Agnes. It was Sister Rosamund who'd calmly served the monks their pitcher of drugged red wine, for they unlocked her cell each evening to cook and wait on them.

Mother Veronica was delighted with all the help they received. Though there were tears and worries and adjustments to be made, she kept things calm and good-natured throughout. Her greatest pleasure was in watching the two girls, Margaret and Anna, exploring their new world.

'See them run!' Mother Veronica caught Marian's arm. 'That is how children should be.'

Margaret, the oldest, was lithe and slim; she ran and jumped around the clearing like the young hare that her misshapen lip was named for. Anna was a year younger, and she loped after Margaret, determined to follow wherever she went, and not be left behind.

'Sisters is the right name for them,' said Mother Veronica. 'They have shared their lives, and are inseparable.'

Marian smiled. 'And Mother is the right name for you,' she said.

Though the nuns welcomed him, Brother James would not stay in the building.

'Twould not be right,' he said, 'now that you all sleep in one room. Besides, Snap and I have got used to the woods. We shall never be far away.'

Mother Veronica fretted that he might get sick, or chilled. 'And who shall take our services?' she begged.

Brother James smiled. 'We are true heretics now, so take your own services. You were always better than me . . . ready to mouth the words, when I forgot the chant. Take care.' He hugged her. 'I go to see the Seeress, and carry her a good meal.'

Agnes and Marian watched him take his leave and go.

'I wondered,' said Marian, speaking softly. 'I wondered about those two. I thought perhaps they were more like . . . well, husband and wife.'

Agnes smiled and shook her head. 'There are many ways of loving,' she said.

As the days grew short and cold, the Sisters withdrew into a hard-working routine. A period of heavy rain turned the forest tracks to thick mud. There was less coming and going between the Magdalen Assart and the Forestwife's clearing, each group of women turning inward to their homes, their energy spent on the hard work of providing food, keeping themselves and their animals alive through the grim winter months.

Brother James and Snap were the only ones who travelled back and forth through the woods, whatever the weather. He carried news and gossip and food to the Seeress. Two weeks before Christmas he arrived at the Forestwife's hut with news that pleased them all. The monks had left the old convent. They'd finished all the ale and wine, and gone. They'd boarded up the doors with planks of wood and notices of excommunication from the Bishop.

'Could the Sisters return?' Marian asked.

He shook his head. 'We must wait. A change of abbot or bishop might see them safe. We must wait awhile and see how the wind blows.'

'Is the Seeress safe?'

'Aye, safe and glad for the Sisters. They have not harmed her but, as we thought, the monks would have left her to starve. Still, Snap and I see her well fed, and she has another visitor,' he smiled.

Marian frowned.

'Aye. Old Sarah spends much time with her. But now I have an invitation for you. Mother Veronica begs that you visit them for Christmas. The Sisters wish to make a feast for all who've given help.'

There were smiles and excitement at that, for their hard-won supplies were going fast with the great numbers of hungry folk that came each day.

'Tell them we'll come with pleasure,' Marian said.

13

The Storyteller

Christmas was a glad time. The Sisters prepared a feast for all the hungry folk who found their way to the Magdalen Assart. There was singing and storytelling and much anxious wondering about King Richard, who had left the Holy Land to return to England. The other ships that sailed with him had come safely to harbour months ago. There was general consternation. What had happened? The King had not come back to England! Was he shipwrecked, drowned, or worse?

Marian sat by Agnes under the strong hide shelters that the nuns had raised in their clearing. The Sisters had been busy providing rough-cut trestle tables to seat their guests.

'Why so sad?' she asked Agnes, who sat quietly amongst the singing and laughing. 'Are we not having a fine celebration?'

Agnes shrugged her shoulders. 'A great feast indeed, but the worst is still to come, and I wonder about . . .'

'Ah! You wonder about that wicked lad of yours?'

'Yes, I do. Does he dine in comfort at Howden with the fighting bishop, or does he shiver with hunger in some cave?'

'Do you not think that he'd find his way to the Forest-wife if he was in trouble?'

Agnes smiled.'Aye. You are right.'

Marian could not stop her own mind wandering to the strange woman in the woods, who chose to be alone. She had been to visit the Seeress twice since the Sisters had left, and found her well fed by Brother James. Marian had taken her one of Selina's old cloaks to fight the winter cold.

Marian smiled as a group of young girls snatched up the hands of the two young novices and pulled them into a twirling dance, but she rose from the table, and picked up her own warm cloak. Then she gathered a fine collection of wholesome pastries that the nuns had made, and packed them carefully into a clean cloth. It was bad enough to be alone all year, but much worse to be alone at Christmastide.

'Brother James,' she bent to touch his arm. He sat beside Mother Veronica looking contented and sleepy, with a mug of ale in one hand and a pastry in the other. 'Brother James, may I take Snap? I go to see the Seeress, and take her Christmas fare.'

'I should go too,' he struggled to his feet.

'You shall not,' Mother Veronica spoke firmly. 'You're in no fit state to stand.'

Brother James wearily did as he was told, and called up Snap. 'Guard Marian!' he ordered.

The old convent stood dark and deserted as Marian passed it by. Just as once before, she heard a voice as she approached the Seeress's cell. She put out her hand to hold Snap back, thinking that the Seeress entertained her foxy friend. But as she drew closer, Marian realised the voice did not belong to the Seeress. It was older, yet somehow familiar. It rose and fell dramatically. A story was being told.

'And Lancelot escorted Guinevere through the tracks and forests of Cornwall. It was springtime. The air was full of sweet smells and blossoms. Guinevere was so beautiful that he could not help but fall in love . . .'

Marian crept close, not wishing to interrupt the speaker. She'd rather wrap her cloak close and sit down to listen, but the heavy panting of Snap could not be silenced.

The voice changed, it took on a frightened, querulous note. 'The trees, the trees are listening . . .'

Marian knew it at once. It was old Sarah.

The Seeress spoke soothingly. 'It's all right, Sarah. 'Tis only Marian. I knew she'd come.'

The Seeress welcomed her special meal, but she begged Marian to take Sarah back with her.

'Take her to the feast, for they should love to hear her tales.'

Marian stared at the old woman, though she could not see her face clearly in the forest gloom. She could not believe that those beautiful words had come from the crazed old woman's lips. How had they overlooked such a thing?

'We never knew you had such fine tales as those locked up in your head,' said Marian.

Sarah did not answer, but poked vacantly at the spikes of a holly leaf.

' 'Tis stories her grandfather told,' the Seeress explained. 'Each word falls perfect from her tongue . . . once started. Take her back, sit her down comfortably with food and drink, and ask her to "tell of the ancient time, when good King Arthur ruled this land." '

'And she will tell it?'

'Oh yes. Her voice will grow strong with her memory.'

So, reluctantly, Marian and Snap guided Sarah back through the woods. Marian doubted still, as Sarah muttered nonsense most of the way. But the Seeress had spoken true. For late the next evening, when the fires were burning low and all had feasted well, they sat Sarah down by the fireside.

'Can you tell us about good King Arthur?' Mother Veronica spoke gently to her.

For a moment Sarah stared blankly. 'That is not how it must begin.'

'Then tell us, dear Sarah. How should it begin?'

'Merlin . . . it begins with Merlin,' Sarah spoke indignantly. 'Merlin was the greatest magician in the land . . .' Her voice grew in strength. 'And it was Merlin who raised the young Arthur, in his secret cave.'

There were gasps of wonder and surprise, then they settled to listen. Sarah held them enthralled. Her stories told them of a time long gone, a time when hopes of justice had prevailed.

Sarah's stories were remembered and retold around the hearths long after the Christmas celebrations were done.

January was the harshest month. The forest clearings were thick with snow. There was nothing to do but shiver by the fires and eke out the food. Still Marian tramped and slithered through the forest tracks, wrapped in her green cloak, to carry food and beg the Seeress to leave her frozen cell. She begged in vain.

Though early February brought a thaw, it was then that the greatest hardship began. They came trudging and slipping through thick muddy tracks . . . whole families of them, the folk who sheltered in the forest, desperate for food. They set up camp in the clearing of the Forestwife, huddled beneath thin hides, or in the shelter of the yew trees. Crying babies, hollow-cheeked children and despairing mothers, begging for nourishment.

Agnes took it calmly for a while. She had prepared for this and hoarded her stocks. Marian was shaken as the numbers grew, and spoke of visiting the nuns to ask their help.

The chickens were slaughtered one by one, leaving only the cockerel and two skinny hens that must be guarded for safety. Then Agnes insisted that one of the goats that had ceased to give milk was killed. Marian found that hard, for goats and people must huddle beneath the same roof for warmth, and the poor ailing beast had curled on Marian's feet each night. She worked her fingers raw chopping up holly leaves, in hopes of feeding the remaining pair. Agnes insisted there was goodness in the spiky leaves, if they could but be chopped fine enough.

The numbers of the hungry grew and the stocks of peas and beans dwindled, till Agnes turned fearful. There were but two sacks of meal and barley left.

'Was it like this in Selina's day?' Marian asked.

Agnes sighed. ' 'Twas bad, but ne'er as bad as this. I swear this is Richard's doing. He drained the manor lords of funds for his fighting crusades. Now the lords drain their villains and serfs, and refuse to feed any extra mouths.'

'We shall go to the Sisters and beg their help,' said Marian.

So Philippa and Emma went with her, and they took Tom and a few of the strongest older children, hoping they'd be able to carry back sacks of grain.

The forest tracks were foul with slush and mud, and the going was difficult. Their despair was absolute when they reached the Magdalen Assart. The Sisters were surrounded by more hungry folk.

'I should have held back from the Christmas feast,' Mother Veronica cried. It was strange to see how lean she'd grown, and even Brother James gaunt-cheeked. It was clear they'd both denied themselves.

'There is but one way left to us,' Philippa said.

Marian looked at her. 'What?'

'A deer stalk. Sherwood is full of them.'

Marian shivered. 'The King's deer? Break the forest laws?'

Philippa shrugged her shoulders. 'What else?'

They all stood silent, frightened by the thought. Then Mother Veronica spoke in her firm, decided way.

'We have no choice. We have good knives that we brought with us, and Sister Catherine has twine to make us nets.'

Marian gasped. 'We will do it. You Sisters should not come. It is a hanging offence.'

Mother Veronica laughed and hugged her. 'Why, when I might burn for heresy, should I fear to hang?'

It was early next morning that they set off, for with the thick mud they must walk through it would take them the best part of a day to reach Sherwood. They hoped to make their kill at dusk, and carry their quarry home secretly through the darkness.

Mother Veronica and strong Sister Rosamund went with them, leaving the other nuns to manage as best they could. Tom went, for a fast runner would be needed. Brother James would not be left behind, though he would not risk Snap in Sherwood again, and left him in Sister Catherine's care.

'What we really need is a fine archer like Agnes's lad,' said Philippa.

Marian frowned.

'Can we really get a deer with knives and nets?' Emma asked.

Philippa nodded. 'We can, if we are not fussy which we take. There is always some poor beast that's lamed or wounded, or sick.'

'Must we look for that?'

'The meat will taste as sweet. We do not hunt for sport.'

14

Those Who Break the Forest Law

*T*he light was failing as they crossed the ancient road made by the Romans, and found their way into the Royal Hunting Forest of Sherwood. With thundering hearts they strode onwards through the stark woodland of leaflorn oaks, that gave little cover. Though there was no immediate sighting of deer, it was clear enough to see they'd passed that way by the fresh hoof marks in the mud and trees stripped of green bark.

Tom was sent ahead. At last he came haring back, waving his arms wildly.

'I've seen 'em. Hundreds of 'em, drinking at a stream, down beyond the rocks.'

Marian grabbed the handle of her knife and caught up her skirt to follow him.

'Nay,' Philippa hissed. 'We must use stealth, and we must stay upwind.'

They gathered together, whispering and making their plans, then, quietly and carefully, they crept up onto the rocks, stretching their necks to see the deer. At least there was more shelter down by the river, with shady yews and holly trees.

The fallow deer were a fine sight indeed. The vast herd

drank and moved in rushes and flurries, so that they joined together as a great swirling mass. It was hard to pick out one poor beast for their victim.

Sister Rosamund pointed and gestured towards the stream. They all screwed up their eyes and tried to follow her directions.

'There,' Tom whispered to Marian. 'Can tha see it? A young stag, with antlers half grown . . . yes, see there, he limps. I think he's been gashed on the shoulder.'

Marian saw the beast at last. Then Philippa was pointing, not at the deer but at a place beyond the stream where two great yew trees stood, then further on towards a rocky outcrop that curved around to form a bowl.

'We must chase him towards those rocks, and trap him there.'

What she meant was clear enough. There amongst the rocks they might make their kill.

Rosamund and Mother Veronica nodded. They all got to their feet carefully. The two nuns carried one net between them, and Emma and Philippa another. Marian drew her knife, Brother James clutched the strong ash stave that he'd sharpened at one end.

They crept towards the beasts, slowly at first, but when the first scent of panic hit the deer, they had to run. Tom hurtled fast and furious towards the nervous, startled beasts, his arms stretched wide. Suddenly their intended victim was lost amongst the many. 'Where is it?'

' 'Tis gone! 'Tis lost!'

'There,' shouted Tom, 'there he goes.'

They saw him again, but wounded or not, the stag had plenty of fight and energy. Twice he broke through the half circle that they tried to form, but such was his fright that he turned and ran towards the rocks.

Tom cheered, and the two nuns ran at the deer, managing to tangle his antlers in their net, but he tore it from their hands. Though his antlers were but half grown, he

managed to wrench Mother Veronica's arm so sharply as
he twisted, that she could not help but cry out. Brother
James dropped his ash stave and ran to her.

Again the wild-eyed stag dodged Tom's waving arms,
dragging the net behind him. Then once again he headed
straight back into the circling rocks. Marian followed fast
behind, gripping her knife tightly, but suddenly a huge
figure rose up growling from behind the rocks, and the
whistle of an arrow sang past her ear and landed with a
great thwang in the deer's neck.

Marian turned her head, stunned by the shock of the
arrow. She was puzzled and dazed by the suddenness
with which the shaft had sung through the air. She could
not clearly understand what had happened, but outrage
and anger burnt through the surprise. All she could see
was that someone else was claiming their deer . . . snatching it from under their very noses.

The hungry children of Barnsdale flashed before her
eyes. The deer was theirs and no other had the right to
claim it. She was the nearest . . . she must be the one to
make the kill and claim it for the Forestwife.

The wounded beast staggered towards her. It dropped
to its haunches, trembling and bellowing through its open
mouth, its eyes rolling wildly. Yet still it struggled to get
up. The fine dappled hairs on its hide smelt of musk and
fear. Marian gripped her knife, eyes blind to all else
around her. She calmly knelt down and cut its throat.

'Nay,' a man's voice cried out in rage. 'No blood!'

Marian staggered backwards. Warm blood spurted out
across her arms and face. The deer fell dead at her feet.

Marian stared stupidly up at the big man who'd shouted
at her, faintly recognising him. There was a distant thud
as another man dropped out of the yew tree. Then
Philippa shouted and ran towards him. It was Robert; he

carried a bow on his shoulder. The big man standing on the rocks was John.

As Robert bent to look at the deer, Marian shouted crazily up at him, ' 'Tis ours . . .'tis for the children!'

'Fool!'

Robert spat it out. But then he stared at her in silence, shaken at what he saw.

She crouched in the forest mud, her face white with anger, though splashed with blood. More blood ran down from her wrist and the hand that still gripped the knife. Her hair was wild and tangled, her long skirt hitched up almost to her knees, showing worn riding-boots, bare legs white and trembling and spattered with more blood.

He turned to look round at the others. Two dishevelled nuns clutched knives, unsure who these intruders might be. A grizzled monk crouched before them, his staff at the ready. Tom and Philippa looked defiantly at him.

'As you see,' said Philippa. 'We will fight to claim our kill.'

Robert turned to John and spoke quietly. 'Look at the state of them! This deer is theirs!'

John nodded his head, and pointed at Marian.

' "No blood," ' I told her. ' "No blood to taint the ground and prove us guilty." '

Marian blinked at Robert uncertainly. 'You agree then, this deer is ours?'

'Aye. 'Tis yours.'

From far away there came the faint sound of a hunting horn. Robert glanced at John.

' 'Twas Muchlyn giving warning, I think.'

'Aye. There's foresters on the prowl, we must go.'

Robert kicked the deer's hindquarters. 'Tha must move this beast fast.'

Marian stared at him, still dazed, though her heart thudded. The two lads turned to go, and Sister Rosamund pulled a ball of twine from her pocket. 'Lash the legs together,' she said.

John leapt up onto the rocks, ready to run in the direction they'd come from, but then he turned to watch their efforts to tie up the deer.

'They'll be caught,' he said.

Robert hesitated, ready to spring up and join him.

'Aye. Caught for sure. A sled might help . . . do you think?'

'Aye.' John leapt back down, and ran to the lowest branches of the nearest oak. He worked a strong, straight branch back and forth, then suddenly broke it from the tree. He threw it to Robert and set about another branch.

'Here,' Robert shouted to Sister Rosamund. 'Fetch that twine, and fasten it tight round here.'

She hurried to follow his instructions. Within a very short time a rough sled had been lashed together, and the deer lifted onto it. Robert swung his cloak from his back and laid it over the deer. The antlers and head stuck out.

He turned to look round at the women and pointed to Marian's green cloak. She did not stop to answer, but tore it from her shoulders, covering the beast's horns, tucking it neatly all about.

Robert pointed to the pool of blood, where the deer had fallen.

'Cover it,' he said. 'Leaves, earth, anything.'

Tom ran to do it, scooping up armfuls of rotting oak leaves.

John bent and touched Emma gently on the arm.

'You must ride,' he said. 'Sit thee down on there.'

Emma hesitated, but Philippa pushed her into place on the sled, on top of the warm deer carcass.

'Yes . . . he's right,' she encouraged. 'Cover it with tha skirt.'

Robert caught Marian roughly by the arm.

'Go wash in the stream, quick! Shift that blood!'

She obeyed without a word, though she could not stop shaking.

John lifted the makeshift yoke of oak over his shoulders, ready to drag the burden, and before long they were off, moving quickly through the thickening darkness.

'This way,' Robert pointed, kicking earth over the first deep sled marks in the mud.

' 'Tis not the way we came,' said Marian.

'Nay, but it will lead us away from the foresters' paths.'

Again the sound of a hunting horn in the distance made them run. John led the way and the others followed. Marian and Robert came last, with many an anxious backwards glance.

It was all the more shocking when a sharp animal cry and sudden metal clang came from the far bushes in front of them.

Marian caught her breath.

' 'Naught but a hare?' She turned to Robert for reassurance.

He stopped. Though she could not see his face clearly in the darkness, still she sensed his disquiet.

He spoke softly. ' 'Twas the clang of a mantrap, I fear.'

John and the others were well ahead now, and it was clear that they'd not heard the cry.

'A mantrap you say?' Marian darted off towards the dark undergrowth from which the sound had seemed to come.

'Nay!' Robert grabbed her arm again. 'There may be more. They set them up in twos and threes.'

'I must be sure 'tis an animal and not . . .'

'Aye, come then. A step at a time, and careful like.'

Deep in the bushes a dark shadow moved and groaned, hunched upright over the cruel iron jaws of the mantrap.

Robert crouched beside the dark shape.

Marian put out her hand to touch the familiar head and shoulders. Her belly lurched with horror.

' 'Tis Tom,' she whispered.

Robert bent over the wicked iron trap. He pressed gently, so that Tom moaned. The sharp metal teeth of the trap had cut into his thigh.

'He's bleeding fast. But the trap is not quite closed. 'Tis a strong stave of wood that's holding it apart. Why, look! The lad still clasps it in his hand.'

Marian peered into the darkness. 'I swear 'tis Brother James's staff,' she cried. ' 'Twas meant for killing deer, though Tom has found a better use for it,' she gabbled on, almost laughing with relief. Then suddenly the danger of it all came back to her. 'We must get him out of it.'

'Nay . . . we cannot. 'Twould take four strong men to open it.'

'Then run and fetch them back.'

Robert put his lips close to her face.

' 'Twill risk us all. Is that what you want?'

Marian leant against the cold, rusting iron of the trap. She wrapped her arms about Tom's shoulders and stroked his clammy head.

' 'Tis the best lad in Barnsdale, and I'll not leave him.'

Robert cursed, but he turned and ran ahead.

The trap was awkward to open, and it took the full strength of John, Robert, Brother James, Philippa and Sister Rosamund to lever it apart. Though Tom was nearly senseless with the fright and pain, he groaned as they worked to set him free. They used their knives and John's oak staff, and at last the cruel trap creaked open. Tom slumped backwards into Marian's arms.

The sound of the hunting horn came again.

'We must go now — and fast,' Robert whispered urgently.

'This leg must be bound up, or he'll die from all the bleeding,' Mother Veronica spoke firmly.

Marian cut a strip from the hem of her kirtle, and set to binding up the wound as best she could in the darkness.

'I fear the bone is smashed,' she said through gritted teeth, her hands shaking wildly now.

'No time to tell,' Philippa cried, as they heard the sound of hooves in the distance.

Tom was placed hurriedly onto the sled, and cloaks thrown over him. John once again set his shoulders to drag the burden, while Philippa and Marian snatched up the ropes that they'd used to lash the sled together. They ran on either side, heaving on the ropes, helping to speed their precious load over the rough and muddy ground.

It was clear that Robert and John knew the forest well, and soon they were leaving Sherwood behind them. It was difficult going, moving with such urgency through the dark.

John plodded steadily onwards, patiently dragging the heavy sled like a great ox. Robert walked beside Marian in awkward silence, though once he caught her arm with clumsy courtesy when she tripped over a rock, and blundered into him. Later, when they left the shelter of the trees, he asked if she was cold without her cloak.

'Nay,' she answered him shortly. But she lied, for as they moved towards the safety of Barnsdale, and the worst fears faded, Marian found herself in the grip of a shaking fit that she could not control. Her skin turned icy cold, and her legs trembled so that it was all she could do to put one foot before the other.

Darkness began to lift as they reached the outskirts of Barnsdale Forest. Robert, who'd fallen into halting conversation with the nuns and Brother James, walked ahead. He suddenly stopped, and turned to John.

'I dare say they may be safe enough here.'

John halted, unsure.

'Aye,' Marian said. 'We're glad of thy help, but we can manage now.'

John turned to look at Emma who lay shivering, half asleep on the sled, her arms cradling the still, white shape of Tom.

'I'm for seeing them safe back, Rob. Maybe we shall have ourselves a leg of roasted venison.'

Robert laughed, and agreed.

Marian wondered if they'd laugh when they saw how many the deer must feed.

15

A Feast of Venison

*T*he sun was high in the sky as they drew close to the Magdalen Assart. Mist rose from the frosted tips of dark piles of bracken. Sharp pointers of sunlight cut down through the trees to touch them. They walked between tall columns of magical twirling mist that curled upwards from the ground, then vanished high above them in the branches of the trees. Emma sat back on the sled, wide awake now, stroking Tom's hair, and watching John's plodding back with an expression of bewilderment.

Marian's spirits soared with the curls of mist. Despite her misery at Tom's plight, they carried back fresh hopes of life for him and for the hungry ones. And Robert . . . ? She looked ahead to where he smiled and nodded at Mother Veronica. Since they'd hastened from Sherwood, and struggled to free Tom, and walked through the night, there'd been no more sneering, no more calling her fool. He was almost . . . almost courteous. Of course she did not care what he thought of her, but . . . it was more pleasant to have him courteous.

As they clambered down the hill above the convent clearing, they were met by hoards of quiet children, who gath-

117

ered around them, staring wide-eyed at Tom, and whimpering with joy as the deer was revealed. Robert and John were baffled by the throng. Then as they came in sight of the camp of shelters, and understood, they fell silent.

John lifted the yoke of the sled from his shoulders and turned to Robert.

'This deer must feed them all?'

Robert shrugged his shoulders, and Mother Veronica answered for him.

'It must feed them all and more. We shall butcher the beast and send half to your mother, the Forestwife. Just as many poor souls shelter by her cottage.'

'This beast cannot make good roast meat to feed all of these.'

'Nay,' the nun smiled sadly. 'We must be careful. These folk could not eat roast meat, 'twould sicken them. We must make first a thin gruel, and hold back the meat for a day or two. Then we may try a richer venison stew, and hope to strengthen them.'

'What then?' John asked.

Mother Veronica shook her head.

Tom was awake, though his face was ashen. They lifted him gently from the sled, and carried him inside. While he groaned through gritted teeth, Marian and Mother Veronica examined him carefully.

' 'Tis a sickening wound,' the old nun said. 'But I do not believe the bone is snapped. I thank the Lord for Brother James's staff.'

'What can we do to help him mend?' Marian begged.

Mother Veronica shook her head. 'That wound needs searing, and the sooner it's done, the better.'

Marian nodded, though she hated the thought of it.

Mother Veronica heated up one of the knives, while Marian patiently fed the last drops of the nuns' elderberry wine to Tom, hoping that it would help with the pain.

Brother James came to help Marian hold the lad still, while Mother Veronica pressed the burning flat of the knife to the wound. Marian gritted her teeth against the smell of burning flesh, and the fierce cries that she dreaded to hear. But Tom was as brave as he'd always been, and though he gave one deep angry growl of pain, he quickly fell into a merciful faint again.

Out in the clearing, Sister Catherine sharpened her knives and quickly set to work on the carcass of the deer. John offered to help, frowning as guts and innards spattered onto the old nun's homespun apron.

'Nay,' she waved him away. 'I have hacked up more beasts than ever tha's seen, lad.'

Philippa hovered at her shoulder. 'Will tha keep the antlers and the skull, Sister? For we must dance for the deer when spring comes.'

Sister Catherine wagged a bloody knife. 'Brother James and Veronica do not hold with that. Heathen rites they call it.'

Philippa nodded. 'Aye, 'tis called heathen, I know. But Sister, when I saw that great herd, drinking from the river, I swore to myself that at least we should dance for them, come spring. They are such beautiful beasts.'

The nun paused in her work, and smiled. 'Beautiful indeed. I shall keep the antlers and the skull. I know how to cut the hide just so. I was once a butcher's wife.'

Robert and John went on with Marian and her friends who carried the wounded boy and half of the deer's carcass to Agnes. This time they were prepared for the hunger that they'd find, but Marian was saddened to see more humps of freshly-dug earth beside Selina's mound.

Agnes was glad to have her son safe and well, though she could not help but chide him. 'Where has tha been, lad? I hoped thee safe at the board of Bishop Hugh.'

'Aye. And so we were. We feasted well at Christmas-tide, but then we thought it best to disappear.'

'Why so?' Marian asked.

'A man arrived at Howden. One we'd seen before. He came from Nottingham.'

'Ah,' Agnes began to understand, but she frowned. 'The Sheriff's man, at Howden? I thought the Bishop had quarrelled with Count John and his Nottingham friends.'

Robert's laugh held no joy. 'This man bears loyalty to none. He may be in the Sheriff's pay for now, but he works for himself. They call him wolf-hunter, but 'tis human wolves he stalks. He kills for money, serving whoever will pay the most. They say he is relentless in his pursuit, and we know that the Sheriff has put a price upon our heads.'

Marian shivered. 'Who is he, this man-hunter?'

'His name is Gisburn.'

'So that is why you left the Bishop?'

Robert shrugged his shoulders. 'We thought it best not to wait and see if we were the wolves that he sought. We shall return to Howden in the spring. When the Bishop moves on Tickhill Castle, we shall be sure to go to fight with him. The Bishop needs every man that's loyal to Richard.'

Agnes did not like it. 'Look, Rob . . . see the state of these forest folk. Why does not tha wonderful Richard come back and see justice done for them?'

Robert shook his head, stubbornly hunching his shoulders. 'You do not see it right, Mother. 'Tis Count John and all the warring priests and barons, not Richard, that's to blame for this suffering.'

Agnes muttered angrily. 'None of them care.'

Tom was put into Agnes's own bed and his mother was sent for. His wound was cleansed and wrapped around with a plaster of pounded bayberry bark and oatmeal, to draw off the poisons. Marian and Emma sat on either side of him, feeding him strengthening wood sage tea, and the thin venison broth.

Robert and John stayed only to make a small meal.

'Will you go so soon?' Agnes's voice was full of regret.

The two lads laughed. 'Last time we came,' said Robert, 'you could not wait to see us gone.'

'Aye, tha were a nuisance then, but now tha's been a help.'

Robert looked around the clearing, at the misery there. He spoke softly and awkwardly.

'We can be more help to thee in Sherwood, Mother. We shall be back within a se'enight with more venison.'

They kept their word and when six days had passed they marched into the clearing, dragging a sled with a fresh-killed deer and a wild boar. They'd carried a pair of deer to the Magdalen Assart first and brought Brother James along with them, and better news from the nuns. Muchlyn came too, and another lad, named Will Stoutley. They were welcomed with wild rejoicing, and a feast was called for. Agnes agreed to it, for the first thin venison stews had done much to revive the sick, and there'd been no more deaths. Tom was recovering faster than any of them could have hoped, and it was all that Alice and Marian could do to keep him from leaving his pallet to try his leg.

At last Marian persuaded him to rest by fetching John and Robert to sit by his side. They told him tales of their escapes from the foresters and wardens as they whittled the new bow staves that they'd cut from the great yew.

Late in the evening, after they'd eaten, and sat around contented and chattering, wondering if they had the strength for a song, Robert picked his way through the gathering until he stood before Marian.

'Will tha stand up?' he asked.

Marian was puzzled, but she could see no reason to

disagree. She got to her feet, and frowned as he set a strong yew stave beside her. Then he notched it where it reached her shoulder.

'If tha must go a-hunting, I'd best teach thee to shoot,' he said. Then he walked away.

Early next morning he came looking for her. He'd strung the bow, and carried a quiver full of arrows.

'Does tha wish to shoot?' he asked.

She stared at him, still surprised, but she answered, 'Aye. I do wish it.'

He turned and walked out of the clearing; she followed him. They didn't go far before he stopped.

'This'll do . . . space enough. Now see, I shall set up a willow wand.'

Marian did as he told her, trying to follow his instructions. He showed her how to take her stance and how to hold the bow. She was awkward and clumsy, with half a mind to tell him not to waste his time. But he was patient enough, and cut a broader wand, moving it closer.

He stood by her shoulder, pointing out the flaws in her aim without the hint of a sneer.

'That's it, pull back till tha thumb touches thine ear. Then close one eye, and so . . . let it go.'

They worked together until the sun stood high in the sky. Though the wand was brought closer and closer . . . still she could not hit it. At last she threw down her bow in frustration. 'I cannot do it,' she shouted. 'Surely 'tis something that must be learned as a bairn. 'Tis too late for me.'

Then Robert laughed. 'Too late? Was I wrong then? I felt sure 'twould be the right thing for thee. When I saw thee kill that deer with a meat knife, I thought . . .'

'You thought me a fool. That's what you called me.'

'Aye, and tha were a fool, to let the blood spill so. But then I thought different. I thought, a lass like that, so fierce and stubborn . . . well, she should learn to shoot.'

She stared back at him for a moment, her mouth dropping open. Was he sneering again? Or was it perhaps as close to a compliment as he could manage?

Silently she raised the bow once more and took aim. He touched her hand where she gripped the bow, raising it, just the slightest hint. Then she let the arrow fly, and nicked the willow wand.

When Marian and Robert returned to the clearing they found Emma and John sitting happily together weaving osier strips into baskets. John was clumsy, his big fingers would not bend to the delicate work, but they laughed together, and Emma reached over to set his work to rights.

Marian and Robert watched them uneasily, both unsure whether they liked what they saw.

'We'd best be off to Sherwood, John,' Robert spoke sharply.

John looked up at Robert, surprised. Then he glanced at Marian.

'Aye, we'll soon be off,' he agreed unhurriedly. 'Tha'd been gone so long, I thought perhaps . . .'

'We'll be off at dawn,' Robert insisted. He turned to Marian. 'We shall fetch thee more venison.'

16

To Honour the Deer

*T*he young men returned to the clearing twice more before spring came. Each time they dragged a good supply of fresh game with them. John's friendship with Emma grew, and the brawny, quietly spoken lad spent many an evening sitting beneath the great oak with the charcoal-burner's daughter at his side. Marian teased them both by calling it the trysting tree.

Tom's wounds healed steadily with Agnes's firm care, and warnings that it would turn bad if he tried it too soon. Though the angry blue-red scars would never fade, by the end of March he was hobbling about the clearing propped on stout crutches that his father and Philippa had made.

One warm spring afternoon, the sound of a hunting horn sent Emma running outside, pink-cheeked and flustered, to find a bigger gang of lads than ever marching into the clearing. She flung herself up into the arms of the tallest one.

Philippa insisted that there should be dancing, not yet to celebrate the summer, but to honour the deer. Agnes agreed, and messages were sent to the Magdalen Assart, though they wondered if the nuns would come for such ancient and pagan rites.

'Will tha stay to celebrate with us?' Agnes begged Robert.

John looked pleased, though Robert frowned.

'We were but passing by, on our way to join Bishop Hugh. There's rumours that the King is captured, and prisoner in a foreign land.'

'Never!'

'Aye. 'Tis not clear yet, but it seems there's talk of a ransom. Count John will think it his chance to take the throne for himself. We shall attack Tickhill, and hold it for Richard.'

'Might we not stay for the feast?' said John. 'Then we shall go.'

Robert agreed, though grudgingly.

Only Sister Christina disapproved. The other nuns came walking through the woods and settled cheerfully to the feast. Mother Veronica and Brother James declared themselves happy enough, as heretics.

'We still give praise to our God,' they said. 'But we shall give the deer their due. They got us through the winter.'

They feasted in the early evening, so they might dance as darkness fell. It was Muchlyn who was chosen to fasten the antlers to his head, for Sister Catherine had preserved them well.

As they lit the candles, the strange horned figure circled the clearing, the tanned deerhide floating down his back. Philippa took up a tabor that she'd made with deerskin stretched on a wooden frame. John put to his lips a pipe that he'd whittled from a branch of deer's horn. It had but five notes, yet the simplicity of the tune he got matched well with the steady thud of the tabor.

Though Muchlyn was small, they had chosen rightly, for he could leap and prance, copying faithfully the delicate movements of the deer.

Little Margaret sat at the feet of Mother Veronica, holding up one hand to cover her hare lip. As Much began to dance, she watched him with wonder, and her hand fell from her face. She reached out to him, twisting and turning her fingers, following every move that he made. Much smiled at the delight in her eyes. He beckoned to her, inviting her to join him. She hesitated for a flustered moment, but Mother Veronica nodded her approval. The young girl rose to her feet and followed Much into the dance. She imitated his swift leaps and bounds with such grace and nimbleness that the whole company watched them spellbound. As the pure pipe music rose and fell, she lost all sense of bashfulness, seeing only the prancing figure of Much, and the magic of the deer's dance.

At last the music ceased. Margaret blinked, suddenly anxious as Much smiled down at her. Her hand flew up to cover her mouth.

'Do not cover theesen,' said Much, gently pulling her hand away. 'Tha face puts me in mind of the beautiful deer that we dance for.'

Mother Veronica watched it all with sudden anxiety, but Brother James put his arm around her. 'Don't worry,' he said. 'We make our own rules now.'

Later in the evening they all joined in the singing and dancing. John would not leave Emma's side, and Much danced with little Margaret. Marian jigged and twirled in the middle of the throng, until she found herself face to face with Robert. He was laughing and merry from the ale. He wrapped his arms around her waist, and swung her round fast and furiously. She grinned back at him, though she could hardly catch her breath. When at last they were both worn out, and the dancing was coming to an end, he turned awkward again, dropping his hands to his sides.

'You go at dawn,' she said.

'Aye. I must get some sleep.' It was true that his face had gone suddenly white.

'We shall dance again for May Day. Will you dance with me then?'

'Aye.' He nodded his head, then he turned and walked away.

When they'd gone, there followed days of steady drizzling rain that turned the forest into a mire.

' 'Tis not the best weather for besieging,' said Agnes. 'Those inside fare dry and warm compared to those without.'

Sparse news came to them from Tickhill, but the whole country was spinning with news of the King. It seemed that he was certainly captured by the Duke of Austria, and seventy thousand marks must be paid before he'd be released. Queen Eleanor had come to England to raise the money for her son, and harsh taxes and demands were made on landowners, manor lords, churches and abbeys.

'Thank goodness 'tis not the serfs and villagers that must pay,' said Marian.

Agnes shrugged her shoulders. ' 'Tis them as shall pay in the end, you'll see.'

Life in the forest clearing went on at the usual busy pace. Agnes taught Marian and Emma much of her knowledge of herbs and healing, and there was the usual endless gathering to be done. As the weather grew warmer they had to search out watercress from the streams, pick tender green angelica stems, and comfrey for healing poultices.

Agnes worked to build up the strength of her few fowls and goats. Soon the clearing ran with cheeping chicks and two wobbly-legged kids.

May Day came and they set a tall pole in front of the giant oak that they'd come to call the trysting tree. Philippa skipped happily with little Rowan, who was growing strong now and walked sturdily. Emma was sad, for there was no sign of John or Robert. Marian was simply annoyed.

'He said he'd be here for May Day.'

'Who?' Emma asked.

'That Robert,' she snapped.

'Ah,' Emma sighed, and nodded her head.

The dancing was well under way when John came alone down the track. He hugged Emma, and told them his news. They had nearly taken Tickhill Castle for the Bishop, but then ruling had come from the great council that the castle was to stay with John, in return for him handing over Windsor. Bishop Hugh had been furious, but he could not disobey. Disappointed though they were, John and Robert had set themselves to help to raise King Richard's ransom, though they did it in their own wicked way.

'We hide out down by Wentbridge, near the great road,' John laughed, 'inviting travellers to dine with us. Then . . . we make 'em pay.'

'What if the poor folk cannot pay?' demanded Emma.

'Why, then we wish them well and send them on their way.'

'Does Robert not come for May Day?' asked Marian.

John shook his head. 'He's mad for his King's return. Naught else will move him.'

Late that night, Marian lay restless on her pallet, though all about her snored. She rolled over, stretching out her arm to Emma. Suddenly she opened her eyes and sat up. Where Emma should have been sleeping beside her there was nothing but a cold space.

'The silly wench,' she muttered. 'I hope she knows what she does.'

John had gone when morning dawned. Emma came creeping into the hut with grass stuck in her hair. Marian pretended to be asleep.

The summer months were kinder to the forest folk. Though there were still the sick to tend, at least the forest was blessed with fruitfulness and teemed with rabbits and pheasants and hares. Bellies were filled, and it was warm enough to sleep beneath the stars.

It was early in August when Tom's mother, Alice, brought the message that old Sarah had wandered off as she always did, but this time she'd not returned.

'I fear I lose my patience with her,' Alice's voice shook with weariness.

'So do we all,' Marian answered her.

Agnes looked worried when she heard the news. They searched the woods close to the coal-digger's hut, calling out her name, but there was no sign of the old woman.

Three days passed and still Sarah did not return. 'We'll gather a gang of lads and lasses to hunt for her,' said Marian. 'And we'll send to the Magdalen Assart, so that the Sisters may seek her too.'

Agnes shook her head. 'I fear they'll not discover her.'

'What troubles thee so?' Marian asked. 'I swear we'll find her wandering as usual.'

'Aye. 'Tis naught but a foolish fear.'

'Don't fret,' Marian told her. 'I'll get Emma, and we'll go seeking the old nuisance once more.'

Marian found Emma pale and watery-eyed, still curled on her pallet, though the sun was high in the sky.

'Why, Emma . . . are you sick?'

'Nay,' Emma smiled weakly, 'I feel sick, but I am not really sick.'

'What then?'

Emma smiled. 'I am with child.'

Marian's mouth dropped open with horror. 'Are you sure?'

But Emma would not let her be angry or fearful.

'Aye . . . you forget, I know how it feels. Do not look

129

like that, for I am glad. I have chosen to have this child. I have chosen the man. I pray that it lives.'

Marian shook her head, exasperated. 'I fear we're in for a bout of trouble. You with child and Sarah lost. Agnes wishes us to search for her, but you cannot go now.'

'Here, pull me up,' Emma insisted, holding out her hand. 'A good walk through the forest shall suit me well. Come on, we shall find the old woman and bring her back.'

But though they searched for three more days and nights Sarah could not be found. Brother James came with messages from the Magdalen Assart. The nuns could find no sign of her. The Seeress was greatly distressed at the old woman's disappearance and she swore that sorrow would come of it.

At last Agnes admitted her fears.

'I think we should send a message to Philippa's husband at Langden.'

Marian stared at her, realising only dimly what that might mean.

Philippa, who was usually so brave, turned pale. 'You think she might have wandered back to her old home? Aye, such a thing can happen with one like Sarah, whose memories come and go.'

'What if she did?' asked Marian. 'What would William of Langden do? Could she betray us, do you think?'

Agnes shook her head. 'How can we know?'

'I shall take Snap, and go to Langden,' said Brother James. 'For none of us are safe until we know.'

17

Can This be the Sea?

Brother James returned the next day. Marian and Philippa were up to their elbows in the dye tub, though they left it at once when they saw the monk stride into the clearing.

'Have you news?' Marian cried.

'Aye. 'Tis not good . . . though it could be worse.'

Agnes and Emma came running to hear what was said.

Brother James had hidden in the thicket close to Langden village, for he'd found that Snap would not stop growling once he'd scented Langden land.

He'd stayed hidden until at last he spied one of Philippa's sons. The lad had told him all he needed to know. Sarah had indeed returned to Langden. She had marched up to her own old cottage and demanded of the new tenants what right they had to be in her home. Fortunately, the young wife remembered Sarah well and the harsh way she'd been treated. She made no fuss, but took poor Sarah in and settled her by the hearth, and there she'd been ever since. The villagers were all doing their best to help. So far, they'd kept the old woman quiet and safe, but no one could tell what William of Langden might do if he saw her.

'Any attempt to persuade her to leave her old fireside sends her into a screaming fit of rage,' Brother James told them. 'But there is more that the lad told me, Philippa.'

'What?' Philippa looked fearful.

'William of Langden has had angry taunting messages from Nottingham's Sheriff. It seems that foresters found bloodied cloth upon a mantrap, and small footprints in the mud around. They say the cloth was torn from the habit of a nun. The Sheriff believes that the wicked heretic nuns have organised a gang of ruffian children to steal the King's deer from Sherwood.'

'Ah . . . 'twould almost be laughable,' said Philippa, 'though I'm fearful of what they'll do.'

'Aye. The Sheriff says that the nuns came from Langden land. He says 'tis William's job to catch them, and he jeers and makes great ridicule — William of Langden bested by a pack of children and chanting women!'

Marian's eyes were wide with fear. 'And old Sarah could give us away to him, any day.'

Brother James shrugged his shoulders and shook his head.

The dye had dried bright green on Marian's arms while they were talking. Once they'd heard the news they could not settle back to their work again. They made Brother James sit down to eat with them, while they went over the problem once more. It was while they were still eating that they heard the sound of hooves.

Marian jumped to her feet. 'William of Langden?' she cried.

'Nay 'tis but one horse,' said Philippa. 'He would only come with all his guards.'

Emma suddenly let out a cry of joy and ran forwards, for a stallion trotted into the clearing with John in the saddle.

He flung himself down, and hugged her, though it was clear his face was drawn with worry.

'Something's wrong?' Marian cried.

'Aye. Something wrong indeed,' said John.

He looked to where Agnes stood behind Marian. He walked slowly towards her, pulling Emma gently along with him.

'Bad news of tha son, I fear.'

'Is he dead?' Agnes asked, her voice calm.

'No . . . but I fear he may be wounded unto death.'

'How then?' Agnes stumbled forward and they made her sit down upon the doorstep.

John crouched at her side. 'That foul man-hunter we told thee of . . . Gisburn. He came upon us down Wentbridge way; he and a gang of Nottingham's best armed fighters. We split up and ran our different ways, as we had always planned we should. Much and Stoutley followed Robert. I wish I'd gone with them, but I went flying off towards Wakefield. 'Twas just three days ago that Stoutley found me and told what happened. Robert headed north towards the River Humber, and . . .' The big man paused, sighing.

'And what?' Marian asked. 'Did Gisburn follow him?'

'Aye. Nottingham's men dropped back and gave up the chase . . . but not Gisburn, he clung to their trail like a rabid dog. That man! Still, he's dead now. Gisburn is dead at last, killed by Robert. He'll hunt no more, but they made a bitter fight of it. Stoutley had gone to Howden for help. He fetched three brave fellows with him, friends we'd made at Tickhill, from amongst the Bishop's men. They were too late.'

'So Robert was alone when Gisburn came upon him?' Marian clenched her hands.

'He and Much. Poor Muchlyn hid in fright. I'm glad he did or he'd be dead for certain.'

'Where is my son now?' Agnes asked.

'In the north, safe in a cottage close by the sea. They'd travelled far with Gisburn on their tails, up through the Forest of Galtres. 'Twas close to Pickering Castle that Robert turned and fought. Bishop Hugh's men carried him across the heather moors, to Baytown, not far from Whitby Abbey. They've friends there who'll protect him. Much is with him, and does his best to nurse him, but Rob has fallen into a sleeping sickness from his wounds.'

John caught Agnes by the hand. 'I have this fine horse from the Bishop's stable, 'twill carry thee and me. We might be there tomorrow if we rode through the night.'

Agnes shook her head.

'I should take good care of thee,' John begged.

Agnes smiled sadly. 'I do not fear to ride with thee, John. 'Tis simply that I am the Forestwife; I stay here.'

John looked to the other women for help, but they shook their heads. There would be no moving Agnes, they knew that. Then Agnes looked up abruptly, biting at her lips.

'Another could go in my place. Both Emma and Marian know enough of healing.'

The two girls looked at each other.

'Will tha come with me, Emma?' John smiled.

Emma suddenly flooded with tears. Marian threw her arm around her shoulders. 'Emma must not go. It shall be me. I'll come with thee, John.'

John looked puzzled and hurt, but he nodded. 'I think there is no time to lose.'

Marian got to her feet, and pulled Agnes up. 'Tell me what herbs to take, and what to do. John, tha must find the time to talk to Emma before we go.'

The women rushed madly about, helping Marian to make herself ready for the journey, William of Langden forgotten for more urgent fears. John and Emma wandered hand in hand towards Selina's mound. When they came back,

Marian was ready, wrapped in her cloak and loaded with bundles of herbs, cordials, and two warm rugs.

John kissed Emma, and hugged her. 'I shall come straight back to thee,' he promised.

Marian climbed up behind John, and Agnes fussed and fretted.

'Take care of theesen, my honey. Make a hot poultice of comfrey. It must be kept hot and freely changed. Has tha heard me right? And you must keep his body warm, though he sweats and sweats. 'Tis the sweating that brings the fever out.'

Marian nodded and smiled, her stomach tight with excitement.

'What of old Sarah?' she said.

Agnes shook her head. 'There's naught we can do. Just wait and hope she comes quietly back to us.'

'Tell the Seeress where I've gone,' Marian begged them.

John blew a last kiss to Emma, then he turned the stallion and they were off, cantering through the woods.

There was plenty of room for two in the saddle. It had been shaped for a knight in chain mail with room to carry weapons. Marian soon grew used to the rocking motion of the horse's stride. The best memories she had of Holt Manor were of riding pillion behind one of her uncle's grooms.

'Does the Bishop send his horse willingly?' Marian asked.

John laughed. 'The Bishop does not know he's harboured outlaws. 'Twould seem discourteous to let him know. So, better not to ask. The Bishop shall have his stallion back, and he'll not complain, so long as we answer his call to arms.'

'Aye!' Marian sighed. Nothing had changed.

They headed north towards Pontefract, close to where the great road ran. They dared not travel on the road in daylight, but kept to the forest tracks that ran close by. At dusk they stopped to eat the bread and goats' cheese that Agnes had packed for them. Marian's back ached, and she staggered around stiff-legged.

Revived by the food and fresh water from a stream, they returned to their journey. As darkness fell, they clattered out onto the wide Roman road. The horse made better progress then, and soon they passed York in the far distance. They left the road, heading east through the Forest of Galtres in the dawn light.

They stopped to eat again, sitting up on a high wooded hillside above an abbey. Below them the bell rang for prime, and an orderly line of nuns filed into the church.

'Could that be Whitby Abbey?' Marian asked.

'I think not,' John shook his head.

'Where are we now?'

John hesitated. 'I've not travelled this way before.'

'Do you mean we're lost?'

'Nay. Not lost, exactly. I know from the stars and the sun that we turned east, and must keep going east, until we reach the sea.'

'I've never seen the sea,' Marian was eager for it.

John scratched his head. 'Nor I.'

Marian frowned. 'How shall we know it then?'

'I do not think we shall mistake it. They say it is like a great lake, that spreads and spreads.'

Marian nodded. 'We'd best get on.'

They rode down the sloping hillside into the valley, and stopped a man with a mule to ask the way.

'Why, this is Rosedale Abbey,' he answered, surprised they should not know. 'For Whitby, tha must head up the valley, then on to High Moor. Follow the beck through Glaisdale till it joins the river Esk. Tha'll see Whitby town ahead, though the land juts out into the sea, so Whitby faces north.'

'And shall we see the sea then?'

'Oh aye,' he grinned. 'Tha'll see the sea.'

They journeyed onwards through banks and hills of bright-flowering purple heather that stretched as far as the eye could see. The sun was sinking behind them when the river widened, sharply dividing two steep cliffs on either side. Clusters of small dwellings clung precipitously to the crags.

'Can they live safe up there?' Marian asked.

John whistled in amazement. 'I swear this must be Whitby town.'

He dismounted, leading Marian upon the horse, open-mouthed, and staring about her at great white birds that swooped and cried.

'See,' John pointed to the eastern side. 'There is the Abbey.' Marian craned her neck to see, but as they walked on she clutched suddenly at the horse's mane. While she rode and John walked, she could see further ahead than he. The cliffs had fallen away, so that the river swelled to spread itself across the wide horizon. Swelled till it seemed to touch the sky. The sight of it made her giddy.

'John,' she whispered. 'Can this be the sea?'

'Aye, for sure it must be.'

They moved slowly onwards, till the horse's hooves sunk into softest silvery sand. Then they paused, staring at the wonder of it. Marian's head turned this way and that.

'I never guessed that it would move so. Like a great lapping beast it is. Do you hear its gentle roar?'

'Aye,' said John. 'And how it taints the wind, with such a smell of fish and salt.'

They stood for a long while, just watching the waves as they crept towards the shingle. At last John dragged his gaze away, to realise with a jolt that they were a growing cause of interest. A group of ragged children had slowly and quietly gathered about them. They stared at Marian with her green cloak and her bright green arms.

'She's the Green Lady,' they whispered.

Marian laughed. 'Nay, just a girl like any other! 'Tis just that I've had my hands in the dye tub. 'Tis forest dyes that make this fine strong green.'

'We travel on to Baytown,' said John. 'Can tha show us the way? We must try to reach it before the light has gone.'

They were set well on their way, up the steep horse road that took them past the Abbey. Up onto the highest cliff tops, where Baytown could be seen in the distance.

'There's men round here who're loyal to Bishop Hugh,' John told her. 'You shall be safe here.'

As they rode towards the first straggling cottages of Baytown, a joyful shout rang out. Muchlyn came hurtling towards them through the falling gloom.

'Thank God,' he cried. 'Thank God that you've come.'

'Does he live?' John asked.

Much's face fell. 'He breathes, but he does little else. I cannot make him eat. I fear he's going fast.'

Marian struggled down from the horse. Much stared at her, puzzled that it was not Agnes who had come. He did not stop to question it, for he was anxious that they should see Robert. Marian followed him into a small thatched hut.

A single candle sent flickering shadows jumping up the walls. A dark shape lay still upon a pile of straw beside a meagre fire that smoked and spluttered on the hearth. The hut was filled with the stench of sickness.

'Light,' said Marian urgently. 'I must have light.'

Much pulled two more candles from the pile by the hearthstone. Marian snatched one from his hand and lit it. She bent down to Robert holding up the candle to see his face. It was grey and bruised, but the skin seemed unbroken. He shivered and muttered nonsense, rolling his eyes but seeing nothing.

Marian put out her hand to touch his forehead. She found it cold and clammy, and he jumped away from her touch, turning his head towards the wall. Then she saw it; a great jagged, festering gash that cut into his skull from his cheekbone to the back of his ear. It stank, and oozed thick pus stained with dark blood. Marian clapped her hand to her mouth. She ran outside to vomit by the snorting horse.

18

The Green Lady

Marian straightened herself, and wiped her mouth, putting up one hand to steady herself against the steaming flanks of the horse. She closed her eyes and took great gulps of salty air into her lungs. The gentle swish and lap of the sea below the cliffs soothed the throbbing of her head.

'I must think clear,' she told herself. 'Warm poultices and a good fire.'

She turned and went into the hut.

'Build up the fire for me, Much.'

'But, lady,' Much hesitated, ' 'tis hard to make a good fire. It is a strange place. They give us all we want of eggs and milk and fish, but they burn this powdery coal upon their fires. It glows slow and steady. 'Twill not burn fierce.'

Marian stared at him, close to panic.

'I must have a blazing fire of wood,' she barked. 'John, you heard what Agnes said.'

'True enough,' John soothed her. 'We shall find wood.'

'And water,' she demanded.

'Here! 'Tis good and fresh from the stream.' Much brought a bucket from the cottage doorstep.

140

'Bring wood then, quick!' Marian gave her orders.

She swallowed hard to quell her lurching stomach and set to cleaning Robert's wound. It was difficult to see clearly in the flickering candlelight and it took a long time to boil water on the fire, but at last she had a comfrey poultice mashed and ready. Robert groaned and shouted when she tried to put it to the wound. Marian clenched her teeth, and tears welled up into her eyes.

'Forgive me, love,' she whispered, and pressed it firmly into place, despite the way he thrashed and growled.

John came rushing in, with his arms full of wood.

'What ails thee?' he cried, seeing her tears.

'Naught,' said Marian. 'Can tha please build up the fire?'

They'd found dry wood down on the beach, above the level of the tide, and soon they had a roaring fire.

Marian set Much to hold the poultice steady, while she washed the sick man, wincing at the stink of him. Then she spoon-fed him with Agnes's sleeping draught, and wrapped him in the rugs.

John and Much snatched a little sleep, but though Marian's head twitched with weariness, she sat up all night, changing the comfrey dressings, keeping them warm and fresh. At last Robert sweated, as Agnes had said he must.

In the morning, Much brought eggs and milk from the village, but none of them could eat. John paced about, until at last he spoke.

'I do not like to leave thee, but . . .'

Marian nodded her head. 'You must go, John. Emma has need of thee, and whether tha goes or stays will make no difference here. I am doing all that Agnes told me, and I cannot do more.'

John nodded. 'Much will do anything you want.'

'I know he will.'

John rode away.

Despite her words, and Muchlyn's willingness, Marian was afraid.

All through the next day they kept the fire blazing, and Marian settled to a short sleep in the afternoon while Much sat by Robert, holding the poultice in place. Marian kept watch beside him through the night.

Though Robert's skin ran with sweat and his body shrank to skin and bones, still the fever raged. Sometimes for a moment she thought he stared at her with recognition, but then he'd shout out for his mother . . . or sometimes for his King.

'Is he any better, do you think?' she'd ask of Much.

He'd frown, and scratch his head and say, 'He is no worse, lady.'

As the light began to fade on her third evening in that place, Marian went outside for air. Much had said she should rest, but she could not sleep.

'A breath of fresh sea air will help me more,' she told him.

She wandered from the cottage, over the sloping clifftop, and down a winding pathway to the beach. She sat down on a rock, and hugged her knees. Despair and panic had been growing in her through the day. The comfrey that Agnes had sent was almost used and done. The fever should have broken, if it was ever going to. She stared out at the heaving sea, her eyes stinging with bitter tears.

An old woman came wandering along the beach, picking up driftwood and filling a small sack with the black powdered coal that was washed up on the sand. As she came close by, Marian wiped her eyes and stared down at the ground, not wishing to be disturbed. The old woman looked at her, and paused, then she came towards her. Marian gave an angry cluck, but the woman ignored her rudeness, and sat down beside her. The smell of fish was strong upon her hands and clothes.

'I heard tell that a strange lady in green had come to nurse a poor wounded man.'

Marian made no answer, but gave a sniff.

'I heard tell that this poor man's wound has turned foul and festering,' the woman continued. 'And that maybe he is close to death.'

At last Marian managed a reluctant response.

'I fear 'tis true. The wound is foul, and will not mend.'

The woman got up, and Marian thought she was going away, but she walked only a few paces, and pulled up from the sand a mass of dark tumbled weeds. She came back to Marian, dragging it beside her. Then she sat down again.

'Hereabouts,' she said, 'we cure our wounds with sea-weed.' She pulled out a handful of the faintly shining strands.

'This? It looks foul and slimy,' Marian touched it. 'Oh . . . surely it would poison a wound even worse.'

The old woman laughed.

'Now . . . if it were my son, all sick and wounded, this is what I'd do. I'd wash this seaweed clean, then chop it fine, and shape it to a plaster.'

'You'd set it to the wound?' Marian asked, hope suddenly flickering in her mind. Dare she put her trust in this woman?

'That's what I'd do, my honey,' she answered, putting Marian sharply in mind of Agnes.

She did not stop to thank the old woman, but snatched up the seaweed and ran.

That night Marian sat up late, holding the seaweed poultice in place. Robert still shook and shivered, but he was quieter. At least it seemed there was no poison in the weed. She thought the wound looked cleaner.

The night was bitterly cold. A strong wind blew from the sea, lashing the waves so that they crashed and roared like devouring beasts. The fire blazed fiercely. She could not make the sick man any warmer . . . could she?

She crouched beside him, though her arm ached and her head dropped from weariness. She glanced at Much, who slept soundly in the far corner on a pile of straw, then looked back with pity at Robert's thin face.

Marian carefully pulled back the covering rugs, and crept in to lie beside him. She lifted his head so that he rested on her arm, and she could hold the poultice in place. She wrapped her legs around his twitching body, and closed her eyes.

When Much awoke next morning he could not see Marian for a moment, and he got up, puzzled, from his pile of straw. Then he saw her, fast asleep beside Robert. He shrugged his shoulders and grinned.

'A fine way to heal a man,' he chuckled. Then as he bent close above them, his face turned solemn with relief. Robert slept calmly. His cheeks were pale and gaunt, but he had ceased all muttering and shivering.

The small man scratched his head, and smiled, 'It seems it's worked,' he whispered.

Much went out for eggs and milk, and when he returned Marian was up and mixing soothing herbs for a drink.

'Have you seen him?' she cried. 'He has not spoken, but he sleeps peaceful. If we can build up his strength now, I am sure he'll live.'

Much nodded, but he hesitated.

'Thanks to thee, lady, tha's saved him for sure. I am that glad he's better, but I hate myself for running from the fight. What will he say to me? I turned sick with fear, and hid from that beast of a man. Leaving Robert to face him . . . alone.'

Marian went to Much and hugged him. 'How can you say that? If you'd not hidden, you'd both be dead. You were there to pick him up, and carry him here. You saved him just as much as me.'

Later in the day, when Much was out collecting wood, Robert stirred and opened his eyes. Marian was standing by the window with her back to him.

She froze, not daring to turn as she heard his voice. It was faint and croaky. 'Mother . . . I had a dream,' he murmured. 'I dreamed that a great stretch of wild water roared below me. A wonderful dream . . . for the green lady slept beside me.'

Marian turned from the window, and went to kneel by his bed. The light fell on her from the window, making Robert gasp. 'Marian,' he whispered.

That night he ate a little coddled egg, spoon-fed by Marian as though he were a child. He was very weak and could do no more than lie there, watching them as they stoked the fire and prepared him tempting food. Marian slept on her own small pile of straw.

Muchlyn brought fresh cod from the village. Marian had never seen anything but salted or fresh-water fish and didn't know what to do with it. She snatched it up and ran over the clifftops, until she could see the beach. The old woman was there, just as before. It seemed she spent her whole life gathering wood and coal. Marian ran down the pathway, waving and calling to her.

'The seaweed poultice worked,' she told her.

'Well, I said it would.'

Marian clutched one silver-skinned fish to her chest. 'Shall I give him this to eat?'

'Aye. That should strengthen him.'

'What shall I do with it?'

The woman laughed. 'Give me that sharp knife from tha

belt. See . . . like this. Cut off its head, then slit along its belly to clean the innards. Now poach it in a bit of milk. 'Twill be the best thing in the world for him.'

So Robert was fed on eggs and poached cod and he grew slowly stronger every day.

There was much to tell him and he lay there happily listening, though she thought he looked a little uncertain when he heard that Emma was with child.

Marian had such faith in seaweed now that she continued to treat the wound with it, and gradually the flesh knit itself together. The side of his face would be scarred, no helping that, and he'd a fine slit ear.

Though he could hear it in his waking and his dreams, Robert had not yet set eyes upon the sea, and he was curious. One sunny afternoon in late October Marian allowed him to get up from his pallet. She supported him to the doorway, where he stood, breathing in the salty air.

Winter approached and the wind grew colder. As the days passed, Robert grew stronger, to Marian's delight, and he begged her to walk with him over the cliffs to glimpse the sea. She agreed at last, insisting that he wrapped a rug about his shoulders. Then she took his arm, and led him outside, turning anxiously to see him blinking in the daylight by the doorway. It hurt her so to see the pallor of his cheeks, and his scar stood out red and livid in the sharp glare of the sun.

'Wait,' she told him, darting back inside, leaving him clinging weakly to the door post.

She took up her green cloak and pulled the knife from her belt. Carefully she cut the strong woven hood free of the mantle, then came back to him triumphantly. Gently she fastened the green hood around his head.

'There, that shall protect thee.'

He smiled, and winced at the pain that came.

'You should not have done that,' he said.

'I can stitch up my cloak, and make a fine mantle of it. Now, lean on me.'

He did as he was told, and they walked towards the sea.

Robert stared, just as Marian and John had done when they first saw it.

'It fills me with terror,' he whispered.

She nodded her understanding. 'I thought so too. But I have grown used to it, and now I love its roaring voice. 'Twas seaweed that brought healing to your wound, and I do believe the fresh salt air brings strength with it.'

They paced along the clifftops, with Much watching them anxiously from the cottage door. Marian moved ahead and Robert hesitated.

'Are you weary then?' she asked.

'Nay,' Robert rubbed his stomach. 'I am hungry.'

They both laughed and turned back to the cottage, walking close together.

'That night . . .' said Robert. 'That night I dreamed the green lady slept beside me . . .'

Marian stopped, her cheeks flamed suddenly red.

Robert pulled her to him. 'Well, it is just that I have often wished she'd creep into my bed again.'

That night Marian fell asleep wrapped in Robert's arms. In the morning Much went off for eggs, as usual, but when he came back, he led a sturdy black-and-white pony.

They both looked up at him in surprise.

'One of Bishop Hugh's men has lent him to me. I may ride him to Howden, and stable him there. Winter comes on fast, and I should go to seek out John.'

Robert struggled to his feet. 'I shall come too.'

Much grinned at him as he tottered and fell foolishly back upon the pile of bedding.

'I think not, dear Rob. You must both winter here. You shall be safe and well fed with fish; the villagers shall see to that. But . . .'twill be a harsh winter in the forest.'

They nodded, remembering the deer hunts.

'Agnes says 'twill be even worse this time,' Marian agreed. 'She swears the poorest folk shall pay the ransom in the end.'

'I'm angry that I cannot come with thee, Much.' Robert put his head in his hands.

Muchlyn squeezed Robert's arm. 'I vow that we shall keep the Forestwife in venison.'

Robert rose again, carefully, and they went to set Muchlyn on his way.

19

The Lone Wolf

Marian and Robert lived together in peace and safety through the winter months. The little sea-battered town stayed free from frost and snow, though the wind was bitterly cold. They made good friends amongst the folk who lived in that isolated place and celebrated Christmas at Whitby Abbey. Marian learned much of seashore plants and healing lore from her new wood-gathering friend.

It was the end of February when news came to them that King Richard's ransom was paid. Count John had fled to France, fearing his brother's return.

Robert was strong and well, though scarred like a fighting dog. Marian watched him sadly from the clifftops as he paced along the beach with his bow, sending arrows whizzing over the rocks. Since they'd heard of Richard's hoped-for return, Robert had done nothing but practise his shooting to strengthen his drawing arm.

She sighed. 'He's like a restless wolf,' she muttered to herself. 'Who could hope to tame such a one?'

She could not hold him there much longer, that was clear enough, and at the same time a picture of Agnes and the Forestwife's clearing came into her mind, and then followed a picture of the Seeress's lonely cell. A strong surge of longing made her smile to herself.

'And I must go too, for I know now where I belong.'

She turned back to the cottage with a sigh, and began to pack their small possessions into bundles.

'What do you do?' he asked, when he returned.

' 'Tis time to go,' she told him.

He did not deny it, but stood in silence watching her. Then at last he caught hold of her and hugged her.

'I have been happy here,' he whispered. 'Happier than ever before. But my King has need of me.'

Robert begged a good strong horse that would carry them both, with the same agreement that Muchlyn had made. They'd leave it safe in the Bishop's stable at Howden.

Marian took charge of their directions, for Robert had no memory of how he'd reached Baytown. They turned reluctantly away from the sea at Whitby, and crossed another heather sea — the moors — still rich with amber and purple hues. Then they travelled on to the Forest of Galtres, and there they made their camp.

They built a good fire, and sat beside it late into the night. A lone wolf howled out in the shadows and Robert leapt to his feet, an arrow gleaming in his bow. He took aim and bent his bow. The grey wolf could be seen clearly, its yellow eyes glinting in the firelight. Marian braced herself to hear its death cry, but it did not come. Robert lowered the bow. The wolf sat down in the distance, still watching them.

'Why?' she asked.

Robert sat down beside her. He shook his head, miserably scratching at the ground with the arrow. 'I shall watch him, as he watches me. I doubt he'll come closer. I know . . . what it is to be hunted. I have more in common with yon grey beast than I do with most of my own kind.'

His words made Marian shiver. She stared across the

fire at him. He'd taken to wearing her hood almost all the time. His face was still lean, his eyes glittered hard and clear in the reflected firelight.

'And now,' he whispered, 'I know what it is to take a man's life.'

Marian stared at him. 'Gisburn?'

'Aye.'

'Was he the first?'

He smiled bitterly at her. 'Did you think I killed my uncle, then?'

She hung her head.

He reached across and took up her hand. 'Believe me, Gisburn was the first, and I would wish him the last.'

Marian clung tightly to his fingers. 'You had no choice. 'Twas kill or be killed.'

He nodded. 'No choice indeed.'

'Can you not give up this fighting, then? Must you still fight with Bishop Hugh?'

He shrugged his shoulders.

' 'Tis all that I can do.'

Later Marian lay awake beneath their blanket, her arms wrapped tightly about him. She was filled with sadness. There would never be another night like this, alone together in the woods.

They wandered a little from their pathway, and went to the west of Howden.

'I shall take thee to Barnsdale first,' said Robert. 'Then ride back to Howden.'

With relief they entered the rough shelter and safety of the great wastes of Barnsdale. They were close to the Forestwife's clearing when Tom spied them from the branch of a tree.

Marian waved and called to him, but he dropped down to the ground, and hobbled away towards the cottage.

Robert slowed the horse to a walk and turned to Marian

with a puzzled frown. 'Something is wrong,' she whispered.

Then John came striding towards them from the clearing. The grim set of his face did nothing to calm their fears.

Robert climbed down from the horse and waited till his friend came close.

'What is it, John?'

The big man shook his head. 'I don't know how to tell. 'Twas a se'enight since. I was making ready to travel north to find thee both.'

Marian sat still upon the horse, her stomach heavy as lead.

'Is it Emma?' she asked.

John shook his head. 'Nay. 'Tis Agnes.'

'What?' They both cried out at once.

'She is dead.'

Marian bowed her head, and covered her face with her hands.

Robert stood stiff and pale, blinking at John.

' 'Twas William of Langden.'

'How?' demanded Robert.

John sighed. ' 'Twill take a bit of telling. Philippa's oldest lad came with an urgent message from Langden, but I fear we had gone to the Magdalen Assart to help them build more shelter for the sick. Only Tom and Agnes were here.'

'What message?' Marian knew the answer.

'The one we'd all dreaded,' said John. 'William of Langden had discovered old Sarah when she wandered from the shelter of her cottage into the spring sunlight. He had her set in the ducking stool, demanding that she tell him where the wicked nuns and the outlaw Philippa were hiding. The villagers were terrified at what he'd do so they sent the lad to find us.'

The big man paused, and dropped his head into his hands, close to tears.

'We were not there.'

'What happened?' Robert demanded, his voice quiet and cold.

'Tom set off to the Magdalen Assart to find us, as fast as he could, but Agnes . . . Agnes broke her rule. She left the clearing and went straight to Langden with Philippa's boy.'

Marian's lips moved slowly. 'She . . . left the forest?'

'Aye. The villagers say that poor Sarah would tell him naught, though he ducked her again and again. It was too much for her, I fear she's dead too. But they say her mind was clear enough at the end. She swore that William would be cursed by the Forestwife. That made him more furious than ever. He had Philippa's husband thrown into the lock-up, and her children dragged from their home. He had them roped together on the village green, threatening to duck them next if nobody would tell him where to find the wild women of the woods. The villagers were horrified, but then came Agnes, all alone. She marched straight up to William of Langden, and she did curse him. They say that he turned white with fear and rage, and had his men throw Agnes into the pond.'

'He drowned my mother?' Robert spoke low, his hands shaking.

'He tried to.'

'Did none go to her aid?'

'Yes, someone did. The villagers were astonished. Lady Matilda came all weak and shivering from her sick bed, led by her daughter. She faced up to her husband and quietly demanded that he cease his cruelty and let the women and children go free. They say that lady Matilda's daughter took a knife from her belt and calmly cut the children's bonds. Then the villagers grew bold with the lady's presence, and pulled Agnes from the pond, but I fear 'twas too late.'

Robert's fist clenched around his bow. 'I shall kill that man.'

153

'No need, he's dead. As soon as Tom found us, I set off for Langden, with Philippa and Brother James. We ran as fast as we could, and Brother James set Snap to go racing ahead. Snap reached the village before us. He flew at his old master and tore his throat. Most of his men-at-arms stood by, unwilling to go to his aid. The others fled. I think that even they had little stomach for their work. The villagers carried Agnes up to the Manor, and set her in Lady Matilda's bed. She lived for two days, and Mother Veronica went to nurse her, but she had taken a lung fever and she died.'

Marian keeled forward in the saddle, and John caught her. Robert stared blankly at them both.

Reluctantly they entered the clearing. They went . . . not to the cottage, but to stand by the newly-turned earth beside Selina's mound that was Agnes's grave.

Emma came slowly to them from the house, her stomach swollen with the child. Philippa followed, and then came Tom, pale and hesitating. Marian turned to her friends, wishing to hurl herself into their arms, but there was something solemn in the formal way that they approached her. Then she saw that Emma carried the girdle of the Forestwife. She held it out towards Marian, offering it.

Marian shuddered and stepped back.

'No,' she cried. ' 'Tis not for me.'

John put his arm about Emma's shoulders. 'Marian . . . it is for thee. Agnes spoke to us, before she died.'

Marian shook her head, she could not bear to hear.

'What?' said Robert. 'What was it that she said?'

Philippa answered him. 'She said that she understood it all at last. That we must not grieve, for 'tis all come about as fate would have it. Marian was ever meant to be the Forestwife.'

Marian stared white-faced at Philippa. 'I cannot. Philippa, it should be you.'

But Philippa shook her head. 'I have waited for your return, but I must go back to Langden and all my little ones now that William is dead.'

Emma offered the girdle again. 'Do not be afraid. I will always be here to help you,' she promised.

Marian lifted the beautiful thing from Emma's hands. She could not look at Robert. Tears poured down her cheeks as she fastened it around her waist. Emma and Philippa wrapped their arms around her on either side, and led her to the cottage door.

Later, they all sat talking quietly. There was a great deal more to tell. The Langden reeve and bailiff had sworn loyalty to Lady Matilda and her daughter, and though the woman was not strong, she'd already made great changes on the Manor. She'd invited the nuns back and begged their help and advice. Mother Veronica had taken courage from the protection that Lady Matilda offered them and gone back to their convent. They'd left two Sisters at the Magdalen Assart, opening it up to any who needed a home.

'They know they may hide in the woods again at the first sign of trouble,' said John. 'Miserable though we are, it seems there's something good come out of this. But Brother James feared for Snap, and he's taken his dog and gone off with Muchlyn and Stoutley to see if they may serve Bishop Hugh.'

Marian stared about her in distress. How could she be the Forestwife? She felt the loss of Agnes bitterly. How could she manage without her? Who would tell her what to do?

'What of the Seeress?' she asked.

'She is safe in her cell,' Emma told her.

'I must go to see her,' Marian said.

20

The Lost Child

Marian threw herself into the work of the Forestwife. It stopped her thinking. It blotted out her sorrow for a while, as she wracked her brains to think what Agnes would have done for every little hurt and pain that the forest folk brought to her. While she worked, she could not feel the bleak and empty space that Agnes left.

Robert stayed there in the clearing, awkward and quiet and ill at ease. Though they clung together through the nights, they had little to say. It seemed they could not share their misery.

When Emma went into labour, Marian was filled with dread, and a desolate yearning for Agnes's presence. She need not have feared, for as the birth progressed, it was almost as though Agnes whispered in her ear, calmly telling her what to do, step by step.

A girl was born, big and strong and kicking. Marian sat back, satisfied with her work. Emma leaned on John, weak with the effort. They both smiled down with pleasure at their child. Even Robert came in to share a little of their joy.

'You two should get wed,' said Marian.

They both laughed. 'We were wed last Michaelmas,' John told her. 'As soon as I returned from Baytown.'

'Who wed thee? Brother James?'

'Nay.' Emma grinned. 'We were wed in a circle of nuns. Brother James said he'd forgotten how, and that six nuns were much better.'

'Six nuns? Is that truly wed then?'

'True enough for us,' said John.

At sunset Robert sought her out.

'Shall you and I be wed?' he asked. 'Shall we stand together in a circle of nuns.'

Marian clenched her hands with sorrow, till the nails bit into her knuckles. She wished very much that they might belong together like Emma and John. It was clear enough that he had feared to be tied to a woman . . . and yet now he begged it of her. She answered him as she must, but gently.

'I can be no man's wife. I am the Forestwife. For me that must suffice.'

He sat beside her in silent misery.

Marian pulled out the length of twine that fastened her mother's garnet ring about her neck. She clasped the ring in her hand, wanting to give it to him, wishing to find some way of comforting. And yet she could not quite bring herself to part with it. She let it drop back into place. They sat there side by side until the sun had gone.

Next morning he took the horse, and left for Howden.

Philippa went back to Langden with Tom and Alice's family. John and Emma were besotted with their child. Marian thought she'd die from loneliness. There was but one person who would always listen, who would weep with her, as she spilled her sadness out into the blossoming spring woods. She took her cloak and set off through the forest for the tiny cell.

The Seeress had little comfort to offer, but her presence and concern always helped. When Marian returned through the forest, she'd gathered strength, enough to go on.

News of King Richard came in March. He'd landed in the south and made his way to London, then headed north to Nottingham. John went marching off to join Robert, besieging Tickhill Castle once again. Emma was sad, but accepting.

They heard that Tickhill Castle had at last been taken, to Bishop Hugh's great delight, with a great army of fighting men who'd come down from the north. Then, later, they heard that the King had marched with a gathering army to Nottingham Castle, where Count John's garrison still held out against him.

Marian came more and more to rely upon the Seeress. Emma was always kind, but wrapped up in her lovely child. Marian remembered the first birth, and did not begrudge her such happiness. The Seeress would listen endlessly, always with sympathy, but also with firm good sense. Marian made many journeys through the wood.

Often she begged the Seeress to leave her cell.

'We could build a new small hut for thee, close to my clearing. I have such need of thee, for there are so many folk who want naught but someone to listen to them.'

But the Seeress would not have it.

' 'Tis a lovely picture you hold out to me, and I long for such a life. But . . . you do not understand. 'Tis for my sin, for my penance that I must stay here.'

Frustrated and despairing, Marian went to visit Mother Veronica, safely settled once more in her old convent home. They sat in the stone-flagged kitchen by a good fire.

'At least we may see the Seeress well comforted and fed, now that we're back,' Veronica tried to soothe Marian's worries. 'Here, sit thee down and take a cup of ale, for we worry about thee. 'Twas clear to us all that you were the chosen one, but you are young indeed, dear Marian, to take up the burden of the Forestwife.'

Marian sighed and sat down to her cup of ale. Sister Catherine brought in a tiny piglet runt, wrapped in a cloth. She set about warming it some milk. Marian smiled at the pink snuffling creature, but still her thoughts were pulled back to the Seeress. She turned to Mother Veronica.

'I have begged the Seeress to come to live near me. Do you think it wrong of me? I swear she would be happy, and I need her so, now that Agnes is gone. You would not think it wrong, would you?'

Mother Veronica laughed. 'I would not. I have long since given up judging others.'

'All she will say is that 'tis her great sin that prevents it. What terrible thing could she have done?'

'I've never known,' Mother Veronica shook her head. 'The Seeress was here before we came, enclosed in her little hut — by her brother, it was said. The Bishop sent us here to guard her, and to take the name of Mary Magdalen's nuns. I believe the Seeress chose the name.' The fat nun shrugged her shoulders. 'That's all I know. She does not wish to tell us more, and I have respected that.'

Marian sat in silence, watching the piglet snuffing up milk from the old nun's fingers, though her mind was still on the strange lonely woman in her cell.

'Though I have never seen her face, I swear she is not an old woman,' she spoke her thoughts out loud.

'No,' said Sister Catherine, who'd been quietly listening to them both while she fed her tiny charge. 'She is not an old woman. And I have seen her face.'

Marian and Mother Veronica both looked sharply across at her.

Sister Catherine blushed. 'I have seen and heard what I should not.' She laughed and gently scratched the piglet's head, 'But then I am a wicked nun.'

'Whatever do you mean, Catherine?' Mother Veronica demanded. 'Most would say that we are all wicked nuns.'

'Yes,' said Sister Catherine, 'but I was wicked long before you. Do you remember that the Seeress was sick? It must be three years since?'

'Yes . . .' Mother Veronica and Marian turned to her, listening intently.

'Well,' Sister Catherine went on, 'I took her food and drink as was my job to do. But the Seeress was so sick that she couldn't even open her hatch.'

'What did you do?'

'I broke all the rules. I opened it myself and I climbed inside — 'tis easy enough to do. The Seeress was shouting out in her sleep. It did not all make sense, but it was clear she sorrowed and cried for a lost child.'

'Ah,' Mother Veronica nodded. 'A child, you say?'

The old nun nodded. 'A child called Mary,' she said, shooting a quick nervous glance across at Marian.

Marian went very quiet.

'What happened then?' Mother Veronica asked.

'I woke her, and I fed her. She was distressed and we talked. 'Twas all against the rules, I know.'

'Drat the rules,' said Mother Veronica. ' 'Twas a good and Christian thing to do.'

'Well,' the old nun continued, 'she was sad and sick, and just for a while all her iron resolution had faded. She told me all about herself. How she'd given birth to a child, a daughter. The father was a sweet-faced minstrel, who'd come to sing to the ladies in her home. The Seeress's brother was beside himself with rage when he discovered their love. He'd planned to marry his sister to a powerful and wealthy man. The minstrel was found poisoned in a ditch. Once she'd given birth to a bastard child, her brother's ambitions to marry her well were over. He'd persuaded her that she must be dead to the world, and lock herself inside that cell to pay for her sin.'

Marian stood up suddenly, sending her stool clattering to the floor.

'What was his name?'

Sister Catherine stared up at her, frightened by the anger in her voice.

'What was his name? Her brother?'

'It was something like a name of a woodland, or a wood.'

'Holt,' thundered Marian. 'Was it Holt?'

'Yes,' the old nun said, dropping the squealing piglet to the floor. 'Yes, that was it, for sure . . . De Holt. The Seeress's name is Eleanor.'

'What can it mean?' Mother Veronica was white with worry.

Marian shook from head to toe. 'It means . . . it means that . . . she is my mother. I am Mary. I am that child.'

Marian ran out of the convent building, heading straight for the Seeress's little wood.

'Can this be true?' Mother Veronica cried.

'Yes,' said Sister Catherine, wiping her eyes. The old nun was pale and shaken, but she spoke with determination. 'Remember, I have seen her face.'

'Did you know?'

'I did not know, but I guessed. They are so alike. I pray that I have done right to speak up.'

Marian ran up to the Seeress's cell. 'I know your sin,' she shouted as she ran. 'I know your sin.'

There was silence from the hut.

Marian pressed her hands against the window grille. 'It is no sin at all,' she whispered.

'Marian?' The Seeress spoke low. 'Is it you?'

'Yes . . . I am Marian. I am the Forestwife . . . but I am Mary, too. I am your daughter.'

There was silence once more. A thick heavy silence and then a small, heartrending cry.

Marian suddenly snatched at her own throat, snapping the silver ring from the thong around her neck. She held the garnet in her hand. The Seeress's fingers came snaking through the gap, and took the ring. She held it cupped in both of her trembling palms.

'Yes,' she breathed, her voice faint and shocked, 'you are my child.'

'Then will you not come out of this damned hole and see me?' Marian cried.

'I cannot! I have sinned against . . . you!' she broke down, sobbing.

'You have not,' cried Marian. 'You gave me life! I am strong and free!' Then her voice dropped, suddenly soft with longing. 'But you know more than any. The one who mothered me is gone and the man I love thinks more of his King than me. I need my mother now.'

Marian scratched frantically at the grille as Mother Veronica and the nuns came rushing into the glade.

Mother Veronica put her hand on Marian's shoulder.

'Marian, stand back,' she ordered.

Sister Catherine carried her meat cleaver. She gripped it tightly in both hands.

'My dear Eleanor,' she shouted, 'do you wish to be free?'

Then the Seeress's voice came clearly through the rustling trees.

'Yes, yes. I beg you, set me free.'

Mother Veronica held tight to Marian, whispering comfort into her ear.

Sister Catherine gave three great chops with her cleaver, and broke a hole through the top of the thatch. It was not difficult, the cell was rickety with age. Then the nuns all set about the hut with a good will. They ripped it apart with their bare hands.

A small, trembling woman stood amongst the rubble, her bed and bucket covered with dust. Marian rushed forward, arms outstretched; she hugged her mother, and rocked her in her arms.

Epilogue

*I*t was May Day, and Philippa had brought her family to the Forestwife's clearing to celebrate. They raised a maypole on the grass before the trysting tree. Emma carried flowers to decorate the pole, her fine daughter strapped to her chest.

Philippa's children ran to Marian, who sat by the cottage door. They presented bunches of flowers to the Forestwife, and to the older woman who sat at her side.

The Seeress smiled, and lifted the flowers to her face. She turned to Marian. 'I never thought to see a day like this.'

In the distance there came the sound of heavy hooves, and the creak of wagon wheels going at a good pace through the forest tracks. Marian got to her feet, fearing trouble.

At last a great ox-cart rumbled into the clearing. Emma cried out with pleasure, for John held the reins. Robert rode astride the ox, his head wrapped still in the green hood.

Marian stared and went over to them, puzzled.

Robert jumped down, smiling.

'We've brought a real ox for you this time.'

'What can this be?' she asked.

164

He bowed, with a flourish. ' 'Tis peas and barley and cornmeal and grain, all for the Forestwife.'

She shook her head in amazement.

' 'Tis a long story,' Robert shifted uncomfortably. 'But I fear I can have no more to do with King Richard.'

Marian stared at him in disbelief. She reached up and took his arm.

They went slowly hand in hand to stand by Agnes's grave. Robert spoke with quiet despair. Marian found his broken spirit harder to bear than recklessness.

He told her how they'd helped Bishop Hugh to take Tickhill Castle, and how they'd then marched with him to Nottingham to support the King. Nottingham Castle had been taken, but they'd had to fight for it.

'Then the King called for a great council,' Robert waved his arms dramatically at the yew trees. 'I thought 'twould be the longed-for day of justice, the day we've waited for. Richard sacked the sheriffs — and how we all cheered. I thought 'twas good King Arthur come back to us.'

'What then?' Marian asked.

Robert frowned, and shook his head. 'Why then . . . he roared and ranted that we'd had it easy. We'd been safe at home while he went fighting wars. We'd been mean and slow to raise his ransom. Now we must find more money, so that he may go to fight for his lands in France.'

'Nay!'

'True enough,' Robert's face was pale with anger.

' 'Tis just as Agnes said.'

'Aye.' He sighed and shook his head again. 'I rage against myself that I would not listen. Now the King has sold the sheriffs back their jobs.'

'What?'

Robert laughed with bitterness. 'Aye, Nottinghamshire has bought his way back into power again, and we may whistle for our pardons.'

'What will you do?'

Robert took her hand, and suddenly the old fire flashed in his eyes. 'I cannot serve my King — I shall serve thee instead. I know you cannot wed, but I shall be the Knight of the Forestwife, devoted to the Sisters of the Magdalen.'

Her mouth parted in a wondering smile. His wild zeal had taken a new and hopeful turn. He spoke with excitement of his plans. 'If I can raise money for a king's ransom, then I can raise money to buy grain. Fat bishops and rich lords who travel the great road shall all make a contribution. Next winter will be harsh indeed, but those who seek the Forestwife — they shall be fed.'

He knelt down before her, wrapping his arms around her waist, hiding his face against her stomach.

Tears poured from Marian's eyes as she bent down, over his hooded head. 'Come, get up, dear Rob,' she whispered, 'for I, too, have much to tell, and someone for you to meet.' She wiped her eyes and smiled at him. 'Look, they have set the maypole by the trysting tree. And though the Forestwife may not be wed, each May Day she shall dance with the green man.'

Afterword

*F*rom an early age I have been fascinated by myths and legends. Stories of King Arthur, Merlin, and Morgan le Fay were full of romance and magic, but Robin Hood — champion of the common folk — was my favourite. I lived close to places associated with him and the image of the ordinary man who fought against injustice, appealed to me enormously. Here was a hero that I could almost identify with.

The only problem was that it was natural as a girl to see myself more as Maid Marian; and I sometimes found that rather irritating. Marian was usually locked up in a castle and needing to be rescued . . . being terribly brave about it, of course. What I really wanted, was to imagine myself running through the forest, along with the men. I wanted to be the one doing the rescuing.

My obsession with the people's hero was revived when my youngest son became addicted to bows and arrows, and *Prince of Thieves* brought new enthusiasm for the stories of Robin Hood. I was pleased that the film gave us a tougher version of Marian, and introduced a wonderful new character in Annie; Little John's wife. I thought that the idea of whole families living in the forest could be

167

taken further. Gradually an idea emerged, for a book that would be much more of a 'Maid Marian' story.

My son and I spent many happy days together visiting places linked with Robin Hood: Little John's grave at Hathersage, the Major Oak in Sherwood Forest, Nottingham Castle, and Robin Hood's Bay in North Yorkshire; close to where I lived as a child.

The earliest ballads are full of references to Barnsdale, which is thought by some historians to have been a forest which stretched right up to the edges of Sheffield in medieval times. All these local connections fuelled my interest, but my search for information about Marian was more disappointing.

Unfortunately the early ballads dating from 1450 contained no references to Marian at all; she seemed to have joined the merry men, along with Friar Tuck in the sixteenth century. Although I had found a satisfying female character in Robin Hood's mother, Marian was central to my idea for the story, and at one point I almost gave the whole thing up.

I decided to turn my attention to women's history in England at the time of Richard 1st. This cheered me no end. I found that while many of the lords were going off to the crusades, and taking their menservants and skilled craftsmen with them, the women were left at home to take charge of castles, manors, crafts, and businesses.

I was also delighted to find records of medieval female outlaws. For example, Agnes, wife of John Sadeler of the village of Ramsley, was outlawed in 1386, for leading a rebellion against the Manor. This gave me the idea for the character of Phillipa, and put my story back on course.

Marian has become so important a part of the legend that I could not leave her out. I decided that her story should represent the real concerns of medieval women. For example: Christina of Markyate (born 1123) refused the marriage that her parents arranged. Despite beatings and imprisonment in her room, Christina dressed herself as a man and escaped. She then spent six years living in hiding in a hermit's cell.

The result of all this reading and research is *The Forest-wife* — a strange mixture of ideas from the very earliest Robin Hood stories, links with my own locality, life at the time of Richard 1st and my interest in women's history. I thoroughly enjoyed the writing of this story and I admit that I took whatever interested me and used it, and ignored whatever I disliked.

Theresa Tomlinson

THE Herring Girls

*T*heresa Tomlinson blends fact with fiction in her moving account of thirteen-year-old Dory, caught up in the close-knit, hard-working fishing community of Whitby. Dory's determined to be a strong, fast worker – but has she got what it takes to be a real herring girl?

Here's a preview to get you hooked...

I took the sharpest knife from my pocket and picked up a good-sized fish, trying hard to remember what Hannah had taught me. I pushed the knife in carefully and twisted it, and the guts flew out into the gut tub.

The man grunted. 'Now size?' he snapped.

'Mattiefull,' I answered him, my voice all shaky.

'What?' He put his hand to his ear.

'Mattiefull,' I said loudly.

He nodded and pointed to the basket behind me. I slipped the fish in and snatched up another herring to gut.

Nelly pushed in beside me and set to work. Mary Jane went to pack the barrel behind us.

I paused to watch Nelly for a moment and my mouth dropped open. Nelly could certainly gip, and she could gip fast. She'd done four fish while I did one.

'Stop gawping,' she muttered under her breath. 'Get gipping!'

RED FOX paperback, £3.50, ISBN 0 09 936311 9